VIGILANCE

BOOKS BY ROBERT JACKSON BENNETT

Foundryside

THE DIVINE CITIES TRILOGY
City of Stairs
City of Blades
City of Miracles

American Elsewhere
The Troupe
Mr. Shivers
The Company Man

VIGILANCE

ROBERT JACKSON BENNETT

A TOM DOHERTY ASSOCIATES BOOK

NEW YORK

This is a work of fiction. All of the characters, organizations, and events portrayed in this novella are either products of the author's imagination or are used fictitiously.

VIGILANCE

Cover art by Brian Stauffer
Cover design by Christine Foltzer

Edited by Justin Landon

A Tor.com Book
Published by Tom Doherty Associates
175 Fifth Avenue
New York, NY 10010

www.tor.com

Tor® is a registered trademark of
Macmillan Publishing Group, LLC.

ISBN 978-1-250-20943-6 (ebook)
ISBN 978-1-250-20944-3 (trade paperback)

First Edition: January 2019

Alone in the elevator, John McDean shuts his eyes, listens to the hum of the machinery, and mentally recites his research.

His Ideal Person is between sixty-four and eighty-one years old. Their average net worth is $202,900, and they are male, Caucasian, and increasingly burdened with medical debt.

Living conditions, he thinks.

McDean's Ideal Person is decidedly suburban or exurban, having resided in an extensive, rigorously planned residential environment (two trees per front yard, gated community, six possible styles of brick) for at least the past ten years, and their home falls between 2,000 and 6,500 square feet—they are not, in other words, "urban" in any sense of the word, and they are decidedly isolated.

Another variable, he thinks. *Marriage.*

His Ideal Person has been married but the number of marriages doesn't really matter: McDean's models indicate that an Ideal Person with up to six marriages under their belt will still generate the minimum target market activation level. His Ideal Person has never performed cunnilingus; or, if they have, they've attempted it less than ten times in their life, and they do not have positive associations with the experience (it just kept *going* and *going,* they say). His Ideal Person has a very fixed concept of domesticity: they have little understanding of how to do laundry, how to cook, how to take care of children. These tasks are unclaimed by John McDean's Ideal Person, and thus, like all unclaimed responsibilities, fall to the wife's domain. John McDean's Ideal Person describes their wife using a variety of keywords—"good woman" definitely sets off a spectrum of psychological framing tools—but the wife doesn't matter. Not to John McDean, and, he's found, probably not to his Ideal Person: when they lose a wife, they quickly go about acquiring another.

Another variable, he thinks. *Response.*

Despite the research on marriage, McDean has seen that the Ideal Person's testosterone, oxytocin, and vasopressin levels all respond just *marvelously* when they see a very specific sort of woman on the television: highly attractive, sharp haircut, steely eyes, bright white teeth, expensive, solid-color dress (Pantone 485 red or 653 blue generate the best responses), and usually blond. She looks wealthy and tough—the Ideal Person imagines her eating shrimp and steak a lot in upscale restaurants.

(McDean knows this from the interviews.) Their paragon of femininity is a hard-driving, outspoken creature, pouring acrimony and accusation from between her ruby lips, a loud, contemptuous, cosmopolitan Valkyrie. In other words, she is a contradiction for them: she is the sort of woman McDean's Ideal Person would never meet and *certainly* never date. McDean is confident that his Ideal Person wouldn't know what the fuck to do with her. Such a woman would expect regular oral sex, surely.

This is what they want—contradiction, he tells himself as he rises. *To see such a person, but not be exposed to her, not be threatened by her.*

A *clunk* from somewhere in the elevator's workings above.

To witness violence and fear, but always from safe refuge.

The elevator begins to slow. McDean opens his eyes and softly exhales.

He remembers all these facets, these features, these subsets and datasets as the elevator silently ascends, past the thirtieth and then fortieth floor of the ONT building. He takes out his tablet and reviews the data like a monk reviewing scriptures. He watches the trendlines on social media, all his AIs and bots sampling the streams, compiling and analyzing the keywords and interactions and impressions. He feels like a sailor before a long voyage, reading the wind as it slices up the evening clouds.

He thinks of his Ideal Person, watching screens in the dark. How shall he wind them up and wind them back down? How shall he "make the needles dance"—the industry term for producing the desired biochemical levels in their skulls?

Will I break records tonight? He hopes so. He's done some fucking impressive stuff with his target market activation numbers in the past few weeks—ad interaction has been off the charts—but that was just normal shit.

Tonight is different. He's going to make sure it is.

The elevator comes to a stop. The doors *swish* open. McDean strides out, past the front desk, through three sets of doors—all of which sense his biometrics and unlock instantly.

He walks down a long, glossy hallway. As the final set of doors opens, he's greeted with an eruption of male voices, a harsh, reeking breeze (smelling of stale coffee, whiskey, cheap beer, vape smoke), and the sight of thousands of white screens floating in the darkness, surrounded by hunched silhouettes.

The control room goes still as all of his producers stop, look back, and see McDean standing at the door.

They stare at him, waiting, trying to read his expression. McDean scowls back at them for a while—and then a smile spreads across his face.

"Hello, boys," he says jovially. "Who's ready to kill some motherfuckers?"

The control room explodes with whoops and claps. McDean strides in and gets ready to start the show.

"There's going to be another one tonight."

Delyna looks up from behind the bar, where she's struggling to unload the ancient, cantankerous glass washer. "What?" she says.

The cook, Raphael, peers over the edge of the order counter at her, his long, hangdog face shiny with grease. "Another one." He leans closer, or at least as close as the counter will let him. "Another episode," he hisses. "That's what they're saying, online." He holds up his phone and waggles it back and forth.

Delyna blows a strand of hair out of her face and hauls the rack out of the steaming machine. "They say that every night."

"Yeah, but it's been, what, four weeks? Five since the last one?"

"They say they don't keep to any pattern. It's random."

"Yeah, that's what they *say*. They say whatever they say. Me, I think it's like rain—get no rain today, then your odds of getting rain tomorrow are higher. Yeah?"

Delyna grits her teeth and starts drying the glasses. She can feel Raphael look her over from behind.

"You carrying?" he asks.

"Never."

"Why not?"

"I know better."

"I'm not sure you do. You're wearing yellow tonight, too? A yellow shirt? That's a target color. People can see you from a block."

"I want tips," she says. As she walks behind the bar, she flicks the big, plastic tub on the corner of the bar—previously a pickle container—and her finger makes a resonant *thunk.* "I want people to notice me."

"Well, maybe not tonight. You at least pack a go bag?"

She sighs. "No. No, Raphael, I did not pack a go bag."

"You gotta get smart, girl. You gotta start bringing clothes that are, like, gray and black and shit. Stuff you can hide in, run in."

"I *am* at least wearing flats." She glances around the South Tavern, taking in the evening's regulars. They are almost entirely men, mostly white, all about forty to fifty. With but a look, she can tell that they are the sort of people who come to bars at this hour because going home is the worse option.

She also notices the bulges at their calves, at their armpits, or the black, matte protuberance at their hip.

All of them are carrying. Maybe they always do. But maybe not. Maybe they're ready for tonight. The only one not carrying is Randy, the Tavern's most-frequent customer, whose chronic alcoholism means he's occasionally homeless. He sits alone in the corner, slouching in his seat, not talking to anyone. She knows in about an hour he's going to stand, go to the bathroom, and only manage to get about 20 percent of his flow of urine in the toilet. Delyna will clean up the rest later.

I do not like, she thinks, *having anything in common with Randy.*

Still, she snorts. "You think they're gonna do a *Vigilance* up in this damned bar? Shit, I hope they send an active in here. Maybe he'd actually tip."

"You laugh," said Raphael, "but they closed off a street in Cleveland and did one there. Just an open street. People running in and out of McDonald's and shit. You gotta wise up, Del, because what you're doing ain't eno—"

"Nothing I do is going to be enough," says Delyna sharply. "You think if I had on a different shirt or some tennis shoes that I'd have a chance? God, Raphael. Trust me. If it happens here, there's nothing you can do about it."

Raphael shakes his head and retreats into the kitchen.

Delyna dries another glass, then glances around the bar once more. There are multiple television screens throughout the seating area, all of them running *The O'Donley Effect* on ONT. Few people seem to be paying much attention.

Delyna grimaces, dries her hands, and picks up the remote. She finds a game—any game, there's always a game—changes the channel to it, and banishes the thought of *Vigilance* from her mind.

McDean begins the evening as he begins nearly every evening: rotating from pit to pit, checking in on each aspect of their production. Each "pit" is essentially a desk with about six to seven giant monitors, before which sits a team of men, hunched over, faces pale and ghostly in the glow.

First up is Neal and Darrow, his enviro eval team. They aren't surprised to find McDean stalking over to them, and they sit back in their chairs and swivel to him in unison.

"How are our prospective sites shaping up?" he asks. He stoops forward to review their monitors.

"The skating rink's performing like dogshit," Darrow says. "Gender ratio is completely fucked. 3.7 men for every woman."

"What!" says McDean. "I thought it was middle school game night!" He spies one window on Darrow's screen and glimpses bleachers full of white men with pale, blocky faces staring out at the ice. Darrow's software ripples over the faces, highlighting each one, tagging them with names, ages, credit scores.

"It is," says Neal. "But there's a dance competition taking place this same night. Alllll the girls are getting siphoned away."

"Fuck. We can't have a goddamn sausage-fest," says McDean. "All-male environments test like shit!"

"That's what I said," said Darrow. "That's why I say not to target sporting events. The gender ratios blow hot and cold, but never in between."

"Why didn't we catch this?" asks McDean.

"Dance competition got rescheduled," says Darrow. "Flu."

"We can tell you anything," says Neal. "But not who's going to get the flu."

McDean sighs. He likes Darrow and Neal, but then, he tends to like spooks. Both came to ONT from the NSA, veterans of some blandly named department whose workings are so classified and compartmentalized and confidential that God Himself doesn't know what the fuck they get up to. They are forgettable men, as spooks tend to be, both small, compact, lean, with deep-set eyes and excellent postures. They even look similar—maybe the military does that to you.

But though they seem unremarkable, both men are astounding mavens when it comes to security, able to carve through systems like a hot knife through butter. Both men have arsenals of bots and spoofed email addresses they can summon up to pound victims with phishing runs and spam until they've mined every goddamn password and credential you could dream of. Since most buildings these days are layered with cameras and biometric sensors (the modern rule is, the only thing that doesn't have a camera in it is a camera), most of which are poorly secured, it's a simple thing for Darrow and Neal to hack in, scan a crowd, and tell you in seconds everyone's ages, places of birth, religions, hell, even people's hobbies, most of which is acquired by the AIs the two have built.

McDean is sure the boys have mined away at him with their advanced tools. It's just too easy. But McDean doesn't give a shit. You don't have to give a shit when you're in charge.

"Then the rink's out," says McDean. "How's the train station?"

"Better," says Darrow. "It's a matter of timing. Depends on which train's coming in."

"Well, no shit," says McDean.

"The 5:15 arrives pretty soon from downtown," says Neal. He points at a window showing a hacked feed from a security camera: McDean glimpses a train platform bustling with people. "And the station's a major junction. Gender ratio's forecasted to be at 1.3, average adult age 43.7, average child age 9.2."

"Race?"

"Sixty-three percent white," says Darrow. "So, decent. Overall, the train station is maintaining a score of .52 on the optimal target map, plus or minus .031."

"And the mall?"

"The mall's a different story," says Neal, nodding enthusiastically.

"New movies out at the theater," says Darrow. He points at a window depicting a feed of a wide, glass-walled hallway, full of people.

"New stores opening. All kinds of shit," says Neal.

"The stats," says McDean, impatient.

"Gender ratio is 1.6, so it's a bit higher. Race is at eighty-two percent white, though."

"Good numbers," says McDean. "But we do too many fucking malls."

"We know," says Darrow. "But it's scoring a .68 on the map. Plus or minus .17. It's a great target."

"Malls usually are," says Neal.

"I get you. But we do too many fucking malls!" says McDean.

"But do your target demographics get tired of seeing them?" says Darrow.

"They will eventually!" snaps McDean. "You two chuckleheads can find another gig mining social media in Buttfuck, Nebraska, but I'm the one that'll be stuck here trying to coax oil out of a tapped well!"

The two men exchange a glance.

"Just saying, boss," says Darrow, "you want to break your TMA stats? Why not go with what works?"

McDean sulks for a moment. He most *certainly* wants to break his target market activation records tonight—but that'll mean fuck all if their audience gets bored with their regular content. "LE?" he asks.

"Environment-wise, two off-duty cops at the train station," says Darrow. "Three at the mall. On-duty, though . . ." He whistles. "The train station is *tight*."

"Seventeen veteran officers of law enforcement," says Neal. "AR glasses loaded with CrowdScan. Same shit we run on the hacked security cameras. But they've also got this shiny new Toronto AI, a developing threat identification scan."

"You can monkey with it, though, right?" asks McDean. "Blind it?"

"We can," says Neal. "But the problems don't stop there."

"The cops have got aug kits with graphene-lined padding, and they're sporting AL-18s," says Darrow. "Semiautomatic and tricked out as hell. Not to mention a small flock of Goshawk drones—four active currently."

"And here's the kicker," says Neal. "All the cops have seen action."

"*All?*" says McDean.

"Every single one of these cops has done some shooting or been shot at," says Darrow. "Luck of the draw. It's just a really mean crew on duty tonight."

"Well, shit," says McDean. "That wouldn't make good television. Our actives would get cut to bits."

"It'd be a short show, that's for sure. We could be in bed by midnight."

McDean sighs. "Tell me about the goddamn mall."

"Twelve LEOs on duty," says Darrow. He sounds a little more animated. "All rocking Klimke 78s—basic shit you can buy at Walmart. Moderate body armor. One cop's seen action. His partner took six rounds, he put the shooter down."

"Wild card, then," muses McDean. "Nice narrative to push."

"We're forecasting an average of 630 environmental participants at the mall over the next two hours," says Neal. "Based on our traffic modeling. That's our peak window—so we'll need to launch *Vigilance* before then."

This is a very sore point for McDean. "Our traffic modeling keeps stepping on its own fucking dick," he says. "When we did the rodeo, it said there'd be three thousand people there! And there were what, twelve hundred?"

"The satellites track vehicle flows," says Darrow. "Can't

help it if rodeo people drive big-ass cars with only one person apiece in them."

"Why are we paying for these fucking AIs if they aren't smart enough to know what rodeo people are like?" says McDean. "Maybe they don't know what mall people are like, either."

"Chinese AIs could do it," says Neal. "They'll just also put spyware in the goddamn toilets within a microsecond of install."

"We got what we got, chief," says Darrow. "Doing our best with it. We going with the mall, or you want us to keep mining?"

McDean considers it. He checks his watch. Just over an hour and a half until the peak window closes. "Keep mining," he says. "I need to check on our actives."

Again, the two men exchange a glance. "You think you can pull a roster of actives who can take on the train station LEOs?" asks Neal dubiously.

"I think I don't fucking know!" snaps McDean.

He's pissed—no, not just pissed, but fucking *livid*. He was angling for the train station tonight, but it's DOA.

His Ideal Person does not want slaughter. They *think* they do, they claim to—but they don't. Despite their inclinations, McDean's Ideal Person doesn't have the guts for modern warfare, and he knows it.

. . .

He charges off through the pits, mind churning, repeating his research like a religious mantra, a bloodless Hare Krishna of stats and ratios and demographics.

Fantasies, he thinks to himself. *Regrets.*

McDean's Ideal Person has served in some branch of the military, or at the very least, they hold the military in very, very high regard. In fact, McDean has studied the analyses and has detected a quiet, anxious guilt within those Ideal Persons who did not serve: an envious, desperate belief that they *should* have served, that they missed their calling, and that if they had served, they would have been an *excellent* soldier, an exceptional but exceptionally modest trooper. Usually when McDean's Ideal Person waxes poetic about this aching desire, they summon up phantoms from the mid-twentieth century, nearly a hundred years ago by now: images of John Wayne and Frank Sinatra (two actors who, McDean knows, successfully dodged the draft, and then made their careers playing soldiers) huddled in the sands of Iwo Jima, their helmet straps dangling by their cheeks, a cigarette drooping from their lips.

A far cry from what service has been for two decades now, all technicians huddled around tiny glowing screens as they pilot incomprehensibly lethal robots through the stratosphere, the civilian structures below rendered in necromantic greens and grays, punctured by a phosphorescent white as a missile makes contact. This is the war that McDean's Ideal Person emphatically supports waging (his Ideal Person is largely for any kind of war, his research shows; it doesn't matter where or why) but it is not the kind of war that they understand, that they know, that they admire. It is not the story in their minds, the story in which they cast themselves as the heroes.

John McDean thinks a lot about those stories.

Focal point, he thinks. *Paternity.*

The Ideal Person is a father, and they think they've been good ones, but McDean knows his Ideal Person feels they don't really understand their children. There is always this unspoken, yawning gap between the Ideal Person and their progeny, this awareness of a sharp divergence in . . . something. Everything, maybe. McDean knows they'd feel this way even under the best conditions, but these days, when so many of the younger generation have fled—to China, to Canada, to South America—this alienation is even more extreme. But McDean has capitalized on this extensively, making sure to use younger anchors and actors at Our Nation's Truth. The image of these fresh-faced youngsters, all so stern and earnest, fills that void for McDean's Ideal Person: he has given them a spectrum of imaginary children, which they embrace eagerly, because all of these imaginary children just so happen to believe the very same things they do.

Focal point, he thinks. *Violence.*

But the final thing, the core quality that John McDean's Ideal Person must have, just absolutely *must* have, is that they must, must, *must* own a gun.

Preferably a pistol rather than a rifle. McDean has confirmed time and again that rifles suggest a very different lifestyle than pistols: rifles are for outdoorsmen, rigorous, confident people who are happy to venture beyond their homesteads—not his target demographic, in other words.

Rifles are for people who are going out to do shooting. But a man carrying a pistol—he's worried about getting shot *at*.

Pistols are for killing people. Pistols are for urban environments. Pistols are for *defense.* They are the perfect choice of John McDean's Ideal Person, isolated within their huge suburban house, wary and suspicious of the outside world, listening to the beautiful women on the television warn them of horrors and depravity in the lands beyond the borders, of corruption creeping into our cities.

Pistols are the choice of the afraid. Pistols are the choice of the *vigilant.*

And if there's one thing John McDean loves more than anything else in the world, it's telling people to be vigilant.

· · ·

McDean stalks through the control room, through the crews of muttering men and flickering screens, toward another pit—the sitters.

"How are our actives?" he asks as he approaches.

Bryce Perry picks up a giant plastic cup from beside his monitor, thoughtfully holds it below his chin, and sends a massive stream of chaw spit spattering into it. He licks his lips and considers what to say. "These boys, hoss," says Perry, "are softer than a fucking boiled egg."

McDean glowers at him. He does not like Perry, his Active Participants chief—also known as the "babysitters department." Perry is Texan (or he used to be, maybe—McDean isn't sure of the terminology, since a lot of Texas burned down over the past four years and is probably still alight), and he's the sort of Texan who really, *really* wants you to know he's Texan: Perry talks loud, jokes louder, and dresses loudest, all plaid and pearl-snaps. But he's good at what he does—McDean imagines he sees in Perry something of a sadistic gym teacher, a powerfully built man with a body gone to seed, but still sporting an eye and an appetite for human weakness. Which is why he's good with the actives.

McDean leans over his shoulder and sees nine windows open on the monitors, depicting live, close-up feeds of nine young men. (Their actives are always young, and always men.) They're all nervous and sweaty, with dull eyes and sunken cheeks. They don't look healthy. Or impressive.

"*This* is who the algos pulled?" asks McDean.

"These are indeed our proud and estimable contestants," says Perry. He fires another squirt of chaw spit into the cup. "They've all trained, a bit. They know how a gun works like anyone knows how a camera works—point and shoot. None of them are formidable. Except maybe this one." He points at one window, where a dead-eyed, blocky-faced young man with neck tattoos stares into the screen. "Gabriel Bonnan. Eval says he's into all kinds of Aryan crap. Iowan."

"Of course." Iowa is overrun with Aryan types these days. The goddamn governor practically goose-stepped around the capital building and off into the fucking cornfields.

"He's also got a nasty rap sheet," says Perry. "All the classic warning signs. Were I to go digging around his yard, I bet I'd find dissected squirrels and cats, that kind of shit."

"Being mean doesn't make you good," says McDean.

"No. But people like to see mean guys go down," says Perry. "And besides, he's the kind of mean that makes everyone's needles dance, yeah?"

"Zoom closer," says McDean.

Perry taps a button, and the window zooms in. Bonnan doesn't blink, he just stares into the camera. McDean is slightly impressed—he knows these feeds are all coming from nine little camera drones hovering in front of the prospective actives' faces, analyzing their biometrics. Being a prospective active naturally makes you jumpy, and having a flying robot in front of your face doesn't help. But Bonnan looks cool as a goddamn cucumber.

McDean reviews the prospects and sighs. "You think these guys can go up against seventeen veteran LEOs, Perry?"

Perry laughs. "I wouldn't trust these boys to fuck a happy hooker," he says. "They'd lose their nerve."

"What are our numbers on seeing someone like Bonnan get pulped?" says McDean.

"Depends," says Perry. "Our target audience demos increasingly have sympathy for the Aryan sort. Ever since the Nazis started dressing natty, the older demos have started thinking—why, these boys seem pretty nice, they're just standing up for their people."

McDean scowls. "Bonnan doesn't look like he owns a fucking collared shirt," he says. "He looks more like a hoodie-and-Velcro-shoes type of dumbass."

"True," says Perry. He sends another spurt of chaw swirling into the depths of the cup. "But seventeen veteran cops spraying the walls with Bonnan's guts . . . that's not going to generate enough threat quotient. People don't want to see a mean dog get put down in the street."

McDean knows this. He's the one who created the models for it. People wanted to see *conflict*—if a guy was bad, they wanted to *see* him being bad, and worry he'd do more bad things. They didn't want to see him just get vaporized like a chump. They'd tune out.

Perry sits back. "They got the train station locked up tighter than a Chinaman's ass, huh?"

McDean says nothing.

"I told you, Hopper keeps trying to get us to target public transport," says Perry, "and eventually they're just gonna turn every bus station and train station into a goddamn bunker. This is gonna piss him off something fierce."

McDean ignores him. "The actives are in position?" he asks.

"My handlers have them twenty minutes away from all three possible environments," says Perry. "Their bodycams are on and feeds are tested. We're ready."

"Good," says McDean. He leaves the sitter pit behind.

"Can't keep 'em on ice forever," says Perry as he leaves. "Some of them are bound to lose their nerve!"

One of the South Tavern regulars orders another beer, and Delyna dutifully fills the glass for him, idly wondering why in the hell this job hasn't been automated. He's a regular, she thinks: long hair, scraggly beard, and an ever-present trucker's hat from some university—she thinks Oklahoma, maybe; she isn't sure.

She definitely remembers his friend: the short, fat man with the dirty fingers, perhaps a mechanic.

"You and your pal carrying tonight?" she asks.

He looks at her, surprised and vaguely offended. "Yeah? That a problem?"

"No," she says. "What's a problem is when your friend forgets his loaded gun in our goddamn bathroom."

"Uhhh," says the man. He looks sheepish. "Oh."

"Which he has done," says Delyna. "Twice."

"Uh, right."

"Let him know that if he leaves it in there again, there's a decent chance Randy is going to piss *allll* over it," she says. She gestures to Randy slumped in the corner. "And trust me—Randy can get piss in all kinds of interesting places. I know. I clean it up."

"Right, right!" he says. "I got it, I got it!"

"I hope so," she says. She returns to filling up his beer.

There's a *bing* sound. The man pulls out his phone, checks his Nuuvu feed. His eyes go wide, and he shakes his head.

"Ohhhh, boy," he says quietly. "Shit. Shee-it." She gives him his beer and he huddles with his friends in a booth in the back, suddenly deep in discussion like conspirators.

Cold dread calcifies in her stomach. She takes out her own phone and opens up Nuuvu.

Instantly, she's bombarded with ads and trends, most of them sponsored. She hacks away at them until she's finally permitted to see her feed. She scrolls through it, and at first sees nothing unusual—just the usual trifecta of babies, puppies, and patriotism, plus a bunch of hysterics about another leaked sex tape—until she spies one post from a prominent media personality: *"where's it gonna be tonight? #v."* This post sports about 18,000 re-ups and over 100,000 likes.

She stares at the post. Like most people, she's come to suspect that about half of the people on Nuuvu are puppet accounts, and some of these are maintained solely to spout propaganda at critical times.

She tries to remember if this personality—some blond, smiling nothing—is one of the bigger propaganda accounts, one that it was wise to listen to.

She glances at the door to the South Tavern. Then she examines the chairs, tables, and furniture around it, wondering how easy it'd be to blockade the door and the windows.

A lot of glass, a lot of exposure. Not very plausible, then.

She looks down at herself—her yellow shirt, her white capris—and wonders if her wardrobe choice has already gotten her killed.

The heart of the matter was that, from the beginning, America had always been a nation of fear.

Fear of the monarchy. Fear of the elites. Fear of losing your property, to the government or invasion. A fear that, though you had worked damn hard to own your own property, some dumb thug or smug city prick would either find a way to steal it or use the law to steal it.

This was what made the beating heart of America: not a sense of civics, not a love of country or people, not respect for the Constitution—but fear.

And where you had fear, you had guns.

You just had to look at the great archetypes of America to see it. Look at the Continental Army during the Revolution, ragged and bleeding and starving and impoverished, but brave and noble—and *why* were they noble? Because of what each soldier held in their hands—a gun.

Look at the cowboys, perhaps that most American of ideals, a lone man able to conquer the beautiful, hostile, empty world with naught but his spirit and a special tool to make his will manifest—a rifle, a six-shooter, a shotgun.

Look at the soldiers during World War II, back when

33

men were real men, true men, and they had a noble country worth fighting for. How did they do it? How did they beat back the tides of evil, and bring democracy and freedom to the world, and keep the forces of fascism from taking away America itself? With a whole bunch of big fucking guns.

The point of being American was that you got to own shit. But when you owned shit, you were afraid someone would take it. But you could be brave, and fight back—if you had a gun.

But sometime at the turn of the century that fear had grown. A lot—in tenor, in intensity, in scope. People became afraid of their own government, their own soldiers, their own neighbors, of companies and technology and schools and churches and other nations. There was just *so much* to worry about.

So, what did you do? You bought a fucking gun.

And here was the beauty of the thing, to McDean and people like him, who quickly spied the trend: the more people were afraid, the more they bought guns. The more guns that were around, the more people tended to use them on each other. The more they used them on each other, the more they were afraid—and so, the more everyone bought guns.

This suited the powers that be. By that point, most of the nation was being run by a handful of people so astronomically wealthy they practically had to invent new numbers to express it. These few people knew that if you said something was for everyone's safety, and put enough money behind it, you could do anything. Most citizens would practically let you rob them blind, right in front of their kids—and they'd thank you for it.

But . . . you did have to keep it regulated. You had to *manage* that fear.

It was the 514th mass shooting of 2026 that had spawned the idea. There'd been yet another school shooting, and some kid sheltering in place had streamed it from his phone. The social media platforms had noticed when everyone had started tuning into it, and then thousands of algorithms sprang into action, plastering the livestream of these horrific murders anywhere and everywhere, splashed with all kinds of sponsor logos or ad bumpers.

At first, the advertisers were horrified. Some random bunch of code had jammed their ad next to a live video feed of children being shot to pieces. That was sure to ruin their branding.

But then they found themselves surprised. Because everyone everywhere had tuned in to watch this horrible siege—and they'd watched for *hours.*

Hours! Actual hours! A-fucking-mazing! The exposure was unbelievable. It was hard to keep anyone's attention for more than three seconds these days.

Afterward, the eureka moment happened. Some congressman—who fucking cares which one—stood up on the House floor and said, "You know why those kids died? You know why dozens of those little kids are dead? It's because we thought schools were safe. Because we've been complacent. Because we aren't ready. Because we still aren't gosh-darned *vigilant*!"

And then someone at the newly founded Our Nation's Truth had wondered—why can't we do both? Why can't we find a way to get everyone to be vigilant, *and* get great ratings?

And thus, the game was born.

McDean skulks over to the next pit, A&M—advertising and media. The sight that greets him is a woman's face, zoomed in so closely her pores look like some distant planet's landscape. It's an amazingly high-resolution monitor, so intense that it makes his eyes hurt. The woman's face is perfect—or at least, McDean's brain recognizes it as perfect. It's difficult to say why it's perfect, but it just *is*: something about the ratios of distance between the eyes, the size of the nostrils, the bend of the corners of the lips, all of this abstruse math that human brains couldn't fathom—but AIs sure could. An AI could parse your social media feed, see which profiles you'd looked at and for how long, and instantly spit out a human visage that would positively drown your brain in a cocktail of potent hormones.

McDean's brain, though, is callused against this particular assault, and rather than relaxing and growing somewhat aroused, he watches, sour-faced, as a mouse cursor zips around the perfect face, altering its coloration, its shading, its pore sizes, and on and on and on.

Sitting before the monitor, rocking back and forth

with a neurotic's classic tick-tock, is Andrews—a small, pale, thin man with receding hair and a delicate mouth and nose. "I know what you're going to say," he says as McDean approaches.

"And what's that?" says McDean crossly.

Andrews makes a few more changes and carefully saves the file. Then he sighs. "That we have algorithms for this."

"No," says McDean.

Andrews pauses. "No?" he says.

"No. I wasn't going to say that. I was going to say that we have *fucking expensive* algorithms for this!" shouts McDean.

There's a pause in the production control room chatter, but it's brief—everyone's used to McDean tearing into Andrews.

"We're an hour and a half out from prep," says McDean, "and my goddamn art guy is trying to make the most fuckable face he possibly can, when I'm literally paying millions of dollars a month for computational power that can generate a whole spectrum of highly, highly, *highly* fuckable faces? Are you kidding me, Andrews? I swear to God, are you fucking kidding me?"

Andrews pouts very slightly. But Andrews is always pouting very slightly, McDean finds. Something in Andrews's face makes him think of a pampered little schoolboy, and it brings out the bully in him. "The algorithms just make a gloss," Andrews says. "I still have to make adjustments. And there are some features that the audience pays attention to more than others."

"Our target audience, goddamn it," says McDean, "is seventy-two fucking years old! They're not going to be able to tell if a pixel or two is out of place, or if the shading is a little wrong!"

Andrews's pout intensifies. "It's just the principle of the thing."

"How many times do I have to tell you this . . ."

Andrews sighs. "That this isn't an art. It's a science."

"Yes. This stopped being an art a hell of a long time ago. Just give me the lineup, okay?"

Sighing, Andrews brings up the windows on his monitors. "We've got the usual," he says. "Dragen security systems, Colt, HK, gold merchants, Procter & Gamble catheters, rest homes, and on and on . . ."

McDean narrows his eyes as he takes in the blur of thumbnail images, all from various advertisements that Andrews's scripts have generated. He tries to suppress his pulse—Andrews, the scummy little pervert, is willing to spend hours on a girl's mouth but barely any time on this, *this,* the feed of advertisements that keep ONT alive. Every day, McDean reminds Andrews that these ads pay for his goddamn bread and butter. Every day, Andrews chooses to fuss with the aesthetics of this or that.

The problem is that Andrews is good. *Very* good. Top-of-his-field good, capable of generating video and audio and imaging of literally anything—*anything.* The sample portfolio that had gotten him hired had included a generated video of Eleanor Roosevelt stripping nude and singing Black Sabbath, this old broad just rocking out in the nude—and it'd been convincing as *hell.* He is a god at generating security camera footage, at lightening or darkening the skin shades of people in *live* feeds, at creating false videos of people one might want to discredit—videos of officials and statesmen and competitors shrieking the most deplorable shit at the top of their lungs, or drunkenly ranting in the back of a police car, or masturbating in a school. Their competitors, of course, do the same—McDean has seen two very convincing videos of himself having sex with an elementary school–aged boy—but they don't have the brand that ONT has or the talent. McDean just wishes that this particular talent wasn't such a greasy little shit.

And he is an *especially* greasy little shit. McDean knows that Andrews has used company software to create terabytes of select portions of the female anatomy: genitals and breasts, sure, but also hands, necks, wrists, hips, dimpled lower backs, the curve of a narrow ankle . . . For a while there he was really into shoulders. Andrews, it seems, does not adore women so much as he adores the components of women. McDean knows all about this because, like every computer at Our Nation's Truth, Andrews's tools are loaded with spyware. Andrews knows this too—he's made a halfhearted attempt every once in a while to clear his stuff—but he probably doesn't care.

Maybe he doesn't care because Andrews knows he's too good to lose. But more than likely, it's because he knows ONT is largely indifferent to this kind of thing. Television and sex have always been intertwined, they say . . . even if the sex is super *weird,* like generating a female face, using a 3-D printer to fabricate a highly realistic latex head with that face, and then holding the head down and fucking its mouth like a horny country kid going to town on a watermelon.

McDean has carefully saved several copies of *that* particular hacked video, stolen from Andrews's phone—just in case the little creep ever gets too ambitious.

"What anchors are we going with? How did Robwright test?" he asks.

"Very positively," says Andrews. "Men like her. A lot. And her scripts are pretty advanced. I thought I'd surround her with men—our core demos seem to like that."

"Which men?"

He shows McDean some anchor headshots. "Gramins," he says. "Bowder. Usual pundit boys."

"That's fine." Then McDean feels his skin go cold. He knows what he needs to ask now. But he doesn't want to.

He takes a breath. "And . . . Perseph is fed in?" he asks.

"Oh, Perseph is fed in to *everything* now," says Andrews. "But you've got your briefing call with Kruse and Hopper in a bit—yes?" He smirks, because he wasn't supposed to know about that. "Kruse can tell you all about it, I expect."

For the first time tonight, McDean feels genuine anxiety. Because Perseph is something . . . new. Unknowable. Uncontrollable.

Different.

"Get the ads sequenced," says McDean. "I want them ready in an hour. Do *not* fuck with me on this, Andrews. An hour—all right?"

"All right," says Andrews, sighing.

McDean suppresses another curse. Ad placement is his specialty. It's been his life's work, tracking the hormone levels of their target audiences and reading patterns for when they were susceptible to certain messaging. If you situate the content the right way and time it perfectly, the human mind is weak to very, *very* specific sorts of communications. To see Andrew fussing with the ads is like a sniper seeing someone fuck with his ammunition before a mission.

But Perseph . . . Perseph could change all that.

Best not to think about it. Get done with the show tonight, McDean tells himself. *Then think about tomorrow.*

McDean reaches into his pocket, takes out a bottle of aspirin, and unceremoniously dumps a few capsules into his mouth. He dry-swallows, then turns to the M portion of A&M—media.

Ives smiles at him, an open, pleasant, intoxicated sort of smile. "Hey, chief," he says. He points a finger-gun at him and clicks his thumb, miming the falling of a hammer. "How's the heart rate?"

"What's going on out there?" says McDean.

"It's quiet," says Ives. "There've been a couple of NFL trades—that's sucking up a lot of the demo's bandwidth. Best bit—another celebrity sex tape got released, and half the people are screaming about how wrong it is, and the other half are trying to find out where to find it. All of them are debating whether it's real, of course."

Ives gestures to his monitors. None of the pit screens have been all that readable thus far, but Ives's takes the cake: one screen is covered with countless ribbons of aggregated social media feeds, another is covered in twelve constantly fluctuating little multiple regression charts, and the third screen is split in two: one half is a fluttering cloud of words, each word tagged with ratios, and the top half is a series of bubble charts, the bubbles expanding or shrinking like tiny supernovae. Reading any of it is like trying to read patterns in car headlights as they fly by you down the highway.

But Ives can read it. This is because there is something very wrong with Ives's brain. McDean isn't sure what—probably drug abuse—but he's always tempted to find out, just in case they need to make another Ives.

"What's the landscape like?" asks McDean.

"Nuuvu is holding positive," says Ives. He takes out a vape pipe and sucks at it absently. A cloud of queerly antiseptic-smelling vapor pours out with his next words: "ImCap, too. What's left of Facebook is still chugging along admirably. All told, we've got 3.6 million brand influencers logged onto the platform and active now. Of those, one hundred and forty thousand are *highly* active. All commenting on the sex tape. Did *we* do the tape, chief?" he asks, genuinely interested.

"No," says McDean. "Not this time. As far as I'm aware, at least."

"Okay," says Ives. "Because it's working out really well. Everyone's tuned in, and *positively* tuned in. Word trends are tilting toward humor, jokes." He taps on a few feeds, which expand like unfurling blossoms, showing countless social media posts: ASCII dicks, kitten reaction loops, the usual memes. A few screengrabs of the sex tape—some actress, McDean doesn't know her—that are blurry enough to make you wonder what's going on. "They're active but unsuspecting," says Ives. "Perfect time."

"And the *Vigilance* chatter?"

Ives brings up a different window and shows him the numbers. "They're anxious. It's been a while. They think a *Vigilance* could happen any time. I put out a taster using a third-tier account, just asking 'where's it gonna be,' and it got over eighteen thousand re-ups. A good sign. Now we're seeing a bunch of boys saying how they'd handle it. Action movie gifs. *Lots* of gun selfies. A few of the subforums are pretty active in how they'd plan a response."

"No one's chattering about the prospective actives? Or the sites?"

"Nope," says Ives. "I've scanned for any mention of our nine prospective actives. Nothing unusual. As for the environments . . ."

"Yeah?"

Ives squirms a bit. "Well . . . We've been successful. Everyone knows any building could be a *Vigilance* environment these days, yeah? But that's the point—right?"

"What are you fucking saying here, Ives?" says McDean with a sigh.

"I'm saying trying to figure out when the chatter is just chatter, and when the chatter is *significant,* gets harder as *Vigilance* gets more successful," says Ives. "My scripts have managed pretty well so far. But it's getting harder."

"But no leaks—right?"

"Oh, *no*," says Ives. "No leaks."

"Good. And you got your bot army all spun up?"

"All spun up and ready to holler, chief," says Ives.

McDean nods and steps back. He checks his watch—almost time for the call. Then he takes a slow, deep breath, and walks toward the conference room.

He passes by the sitter pit and glances over Perry's broad shoulders at his screen. He sees the nine young men there, nervous and trembling and sweating, all save Bonnan, who is as placid as a Hindu fucking cow. McDean's heart skips a beat—not with disgust but rather excitement.

He imagines Bonnan walking into an office building, maybe in a black longcoat with military fatigues. He imagines the boy raising his assault rifle and opening up on the unsuspecting workers, his fully automatic weapon chewing through the desks, the walls, and, of course, the people cowering behind their cover, screaming as the rounds tear the world apart . . .

I like that boy, he thinks. *He's going to make some great fucking TMA stats.*

He walks into the conference room.

The game was simple—in broad strokes, at least.

Potential contestants went on the ONT website and filled out a form. It was probably the most intense contract ever created in history, largely generated by legal AIs that could cover your ass *literally* a million times better than any high-priced law firm. ONT was great at goosing submissions to the form: they had ads on depression forums and sites frequented by people with psychological issues, all solid fodder for *Vigilance.*

Once the potential contestants had filled out the form, they were put into a huge pool of people, hundreds of thousands, and told: *We have your phone number. Keep it on at all times. We can call at any moment, anywhere. You miss the call, you're out.*

Then the potential contestants waited. Sometimes they forgot about it. Most didn't. You didn't forget that you'd submitted yourself for that kind of thing.

Then, at the discretion of McDean and ONT, the *Vigilance* clock would suddenly start ticking.

Calibrated AIs and black box software would select the possible locations for the *Vigilance* environment. Algorithms picked the first cull of possible actives from the submission pool—usually thirty or so people. Then the possible actives got culled more, based on proximity and relation to those environments—did they know the place? Were they familiar with it? Was it completely unknown to them? This group—usually about a dozen people—would get contacted immediately and told they were on deck: *You have been selected as a possible competitor in an upcoming* Vigilance. *Please proceed to the following coordinates for pickup.*

A crew of *Vigilance* handlers—all coordinated by Bryce Perry, lord of the babysitters—would descend, swoop up the potential active shooters, and pack them into circling unmarked vans. Then they'd get studied by the *Vigilance* producing team to make sure they were just, just, *just* right for the upcoming environment.

It was impossible to express how calculated all this was. ONT knew every possible thing about their most lucrative audience member, McDean's Ideal Person: what they liked, what they hated, how long they slept, how many times they'd fucked—and what they wanted to see. They selected prospective *Vigilance* environments specifically to appeal to the audience, and they selected prospective actives based on the environments and the audience. It was essentially like filling in a very, very complicated equation. And when you had all the values filled in . . .

You made your choice, and selected the final environment.

The environments were the hardest part. The people inside the buildings could have *no* possible inkling that they were about to be subjected to *Vigilance.* To do so would spoil the game, which would damage the TMAs, which would hurt advertising numbers. And you also wanted the environments to be *right.* You didn't want to have an all-male environment, or all-female, or just kids, or the wrong race or income levels or professions. It had to have *broad* appeal.

You were creating a story that every audience member would cast themselves in—and the allure came from watching to see if they'd survive.

Once the environment was selected, the final selection of actives was made. You wanted usually at least two active shooters for every *Vigilance* environment. One shooter was boring, and anything north of six was confusing for the audience—like everything else in ONT, this had been carefully studied. The average was 3.47 shooters per *Vigilance.*

Once your active shooters were selected, the unselected were given some compensatory fee—usually $500 or so—and then dropped off back at home: "Thanks but no thanks, fuck off." Then came prep time: the selected actives were suited up with bodycams and given one thousand "gear points." Then the boxes of gear in the *Vigi-*

lance vans were thrown open, and the active shooters had to make their choice.

An AL-18—a highly efficient, beautifully lethal assault rifle—cost 800 points. So, nearly all of them. A Klimke 78—basic police-issue pistol—cost 350. An extended clip for either firearm cost 100. Scoped hunting rifle—that cost 550. Body armor also cost 550 points, enough to make it undesirable. (*Vigilance* was not a game in which hedging your risks was encouraged.) Grenades cost 200 apiece. A better entrance cost 250. Stims that would amp up your reaction time cost 100 a dose. And so on, and so on, and so on.

Ammunition was free, of course, including hollowpoints and armor-piercing rounds. *Shoot all you'd like,* they said. *That's the point.*

Once the gear had been selected, each active shooter was taken to their assigned (or chosen, if they'd spent the points) entrance, where they waited until the light went green.

The *Vigilance* production team waited until the perfect possible moment—and then all the active shooters were introduced into the *Vigilance* environment.

The environment was locked down by ONT security. And what happened next . . .

Well. That was some great fucking television.

If a shooter died—which was very, very likely—their

listed contacts were compensated with one million dollars.

If a civilian or a law enforcement officer took out a shooter, they were rewarded with five million dollars.

And if a shooter survived *Vigilance*—in other words, if they were the final lone survivor, with no civilians, no LEOs, and no other shooter possessing a pulse in the *Vigilance* environment—they were awarded with the grand prize, twenty million dollars.

So far, ONT had only had to give out the grand prize twice. Both times, the active shooters had been unusually proficient, and the *Vigilance* production team had adjusted the metrics to make sure that sort of person never got selected again.

Now, the obvious fucking question was—why would civilians agree to this? Why consent to the possibility that you might be gunned down for pure entertainment?

The first answer to that was easy: America was dying. Quite literally. There'd been a mass migration of the younger generations and immigrants out of America throughout the 2020s, leaving the nation saddled with an older generation that couldn't work but was entitled to steadily advancing medical technology that kept them all alive for far longer than any economist had ever predicted. The elderly population ate up whatever national budgets remained like locusts devouring corn in the fields—there were no funds for roads, bridges, schools, and definitely no money to deal with all the floods and fires and droughts that kept happening. America stopped doing nearly everything.

Except television. America's aging population might not be able to work, but they sure as fuck could watch some television.

So, ONT went to various places in America—malls, offices, schools, public transit—and said, "Hey. You're broke, and you're already getting subjected to mass shootings—that's just part of living in fucking America, okay? But here's the deal—we subject you to our *controlled* mass shootings, we stream it over multiple platforms, and you get a cut of our ad revenue."

Almost every place had consented. All they had to do was put up a sign at the entrances and exits saying: THIS FACILITY CAN BE SUBJECT TO OUR NATION'S TRUTH'S VIGILANCE™ AT ANY MOMENT, with a lot of fine print indicating that, if you walked in, you were agreeing to the contract—i.e., you couldn't sue their ass off if your brother or wife or kid got blown away on national television.

So, that was the first answer, which was easy to explain. But the second answer . . . that was harder.

Because, to ONT's surprise, people *wanted* to be civilians in *Vigilance*. They wanted to be bystanders, to be attacked. They wanted to be under siege. They wanted to stand up, and fight back, and see if they survived.

This had been goddamn puzzling for McDean and his crew. What idiot, what fucking *moron* could possibly be not just willing but *eager* to get shot at by a well-armed loon?

Yet the answer seemed to be—Americans. Lots of Americans. *Most* Americans, in fact.

It'd taken McDean some time to figure it out. Since the turn of the century, America's media had been constantly telling Americans that they weren't safe, because that was what people wanted to hear: the human brain had evolved to prioritize threats, so they instantly migrated to them. This meant the news gave them all the threats they could have possibly wanted to hear—anything for a click or a ratings bump.

Eventually, Americans had gotten so conditioned that they couldn't conceive of an America *without* constant danger. They saw people shooting on the news, screaming on the news, dying on the news, and they'd started to believe—*this is just ordinary life.* And it was up to you to deal with it.

Which generally explains how people react to *Vigilance.* If you're an American, and you hear someone you know or love got wiped out on McDean's show, your response isn't "How on Earth can ONT be allowed to kill our own citizens?"

Instead, it's "Why didn't that dumb fuck have a gun and shoot back? Why wasn't he prepared? Why wasn't he *vigilant*?"

More than anyone alive, John McDean knows America isn't a place you live in—not anymore. It's a place you *survive*. And such a place is highly monetizable for Our Nation's Truth.

Business at the South Tavern was already at a crawl, but with the looming specter of an impending *Vigilance,* it abruptly and thoroughly dies.

"Maybe a good thing," says Raphael's voice softly over her shoulder. "All these boys going to be trapped in here. Ain't no one going out tonight."

"Maybe."

"I think this happened before. They gonna buy a lot of beer and tip like fools." He sniffs.

"I don't want Randy sleeping here tonight," she says, eyeing him slumped in the corner.

"Randy gonna Randy," says Raphael. "Not much you can do about that."

Together they glance out at the street and see it rapidly emptying. "But it could be good," he continues. Then he adds, "Provided it don't happen here."

Delyna looks over the South Tavern regulars and suddenly feels that this is not at all a good thing. They are mostly all white, frustrated, drunk, and armed—a combination that would make any unarmed black woman uneasy.

But she knows that even if she were armed, she'd find little solace in it. Delyna took many lessons from her father, but the ones he taught on firearms burn bright in her mind these days.

So, you have a gun. But having a gun doesn't make you a decent shooter any more than holding a football makes you a damn quarterback. Once you got it—do you train with it? Every week? Take classes? Clean it, care for it, maintain it, and train some more? Even then, do you really think you'll be equipped to act lethally with it? Who knows? A gun is just a tool, Delyna. It's like a hammer or a saw. Its use is more here—he'd tapped the side of his head then—*than here,* he said, holding up his trigger finger, crooking the knuckles. Then he'd dropped into cop-speech: *To use a firearm wisely is about training to be cognizant of your environment and those moving within it, and learning the decision paths that lead you to use that firearm. A firearm should provoke analysis and thought, not action. Or that's how it should be, at least. But thinkin' is something more and more people seem goddamn reluctant to do these days.*

She remembers how he looked as he gave that speech, sitting on the edge of his bed with his shoes off, his uniform shirt unbuttoned. As a young girl, she'd always imagined her father more as a divine force than a man, especially when he wore the uniform. Those moments of almost forbidden vulnerability stay close with her now.

She remembers the sound of that knock in the night. Her mother's footsteps, the creak of the door. Then the dreadful wailing.

As a child, Delyna had always been vaguely aware that her father might get killed in the line of duty. Yet it had never, ever, *ever* occurred to her that he might get shot and killed by another cop. But that was how it'd gone down: a botched collar, a chase through dark streets, some police officer peering into the shadows and spying the silhouette of a man with a gun—maybe a black man with a gun?—and lighting him up.

The police department paid her family a good bit of money and sternly warned them not to sue. The officer who did the shooting was suspended but not fired.

Delyna's mother took the hint. They moved away and tried to forget.

Delyna is still trying.

She stands behind the bar and watches the white boys twitch and whisper and softly whoop as they discuss what's coming, playing out lethal fantasies in their minds.

She doesn't regret not having a gun tonight. Her father's life had taught her that the odds of her doing any good with it were miserably low, and the odds of it getting her killed were very, very high.

McDean walks into the conference room, and instantly the monitors inside flick on. Tiny cameras in the corners read his face, his movements, and identify him; then the monitors communicate with the ONT calendars, find his appointment, and start the video call, all without him doing a thing or saying a word.

McDean sits and watches as the cartoonish ONT video-call logo pops up and bounces around on the screens, waiting for someone on the other end to pick up. He watches it like a cat watching a goldfish bob around in a tank.

He hates this. He hates talking to Hopper and Kruse. It's like summoning the dead—and, in some ways, it almost really is.

There's a pleasant *bloop!* sound. McDean looks up, and one of the monitors switches abruptly to a feed of what looks like a corpse in a hospital bed.

The corpse is fat and bulging, especially around the arms and hips, and it has countless tubes running into its graying, wrinkled body, into its arms, its neck, its ears. The corpse wears a specially made piece of hospital clothing to cover up most of its torso and its genitals—if it even has any anymore, McDean isn't sure. A huge plastic mask covered in blinking buttons conceals the lower half of its face—this component is an especially dense network of tubes.

Then the chest twitches. The corpse's trembling hand rises, and it gently tugs the mask away, revealing a quivering, wet mouth full of yellow teeth. The corpse coughs and bellows in a raspy, country twang: "God*damn* it, McDean! I'm gettin' trickles that you ain't gonna go for the goddamn train station, and I swear to fuckin' Christ, boy, I do *not* want to hear that shit!"

"Good evening, Mr. Hopper," says McDean calmly. McDean isn't surprised to discover Hopper's already heard how they're leaning. Bryce Perry is a favorite of Hopper's, so usually everything Perry hears finds its way back to Hopper eventually.

"Don't you fuckin' *good evening* me," snaps Hopper, "you greasy little marketing shit! This is gonna be the fourth *Vigilance* in a fuckin' row that don't do what I fuckin' want it to do!"

"We've studied the environment, a—"

"Studied how? With your goddamn heads stuffed so far up your goddamn asses that you could kiss your fuckin' livers?"

" . . . and the metrics are not looking great on the train

station as a *Vigilance* environment," says McDean. "The law enforcement presence there is simply overwhelming."

"Then hire soldiers!" snarls Hopper. "Real ones! Put on a good goddamn show!"

"Other ONT affiliates have tried that," says McDean. "It significantly hurt TMAs. We're not sure how—we've dedicated hours of study to this, though so far the results have been inconclusive—but our core demographics can tell when the shooters or shooting is inauthentic. And they do not like it."

"You mean we can generate anything under the fuckin' sun *except* a dumbass with a rifle?" asks Hopper.

"It seems," says McDean evenly, "that there are still limits to the technology. And there are second-order effects, too. Real shooters from real life generate far more social media buzz than someone groomed or planted. It's a *very* powerful branding exercise, with lasting, durable market impressions, the value of which totals in the billions."

Hopper glares into the ceiling as he considers it. "Fuckin' television," he says. "Sometimes I wished I kept my ass in oil."

McDean frankly wishes the same. Wayne Hogget Hopper is perhaps the last remaining oil tycoon in the nation, if not the world. It was Hopper who pioneered the development of the autonomous frack rig, a massive behemoth of a robot that mindlessly trundles across the West, sensing oil and gas buried in the earth and extracting it like a giant, billion-dollar mosquito. That's the only way to get oil out of America anymore, since so much of the land keeps burning.

But the world is not interested in America's oil anymore. China banned all internal combustion engines in the late 2020s, and Europe and India and the rest of the world followed suit soon after. All of this, of course, was made possible by China's advanced factories, which pumped out electric cars, self-driving electric cars, and even self-driving *flying* electric cars.

They definitely don't have any of those in America. Mostly due to Hopper, and men like him, who went well out of their way to block such technologies. Though he's one of ONT's major shareholders, Hopper remains an oil man at heart, and he's intent on seeing America keep using it. Hence his desire to see train stations and public transit get attacked in every *Vigilance*.

McDean doesn't understand the source of this desire, really. Hopper is both very, very wealthy, and very, very dying. Why a dollar more or a barrel more of oil matters to him is beyond the inkling of marketing men like McDean. Maybe that was just capitalism—always expanding, even in death. Or maybe this world simply belongs to men like Hopper, and always would, even in their death throes.

"So, what the hell you goin' to do, then?" asks Hopper.

"We're looking at a mall," says McDean.

"A mall? *Again?*"

"It scores very highly on the target map."

"Why don't we just do a fuckin' rerun, then?" says Hopper. "Do they still do those on your streaming platform or whatever you call it?"

"We'll know our situation when we see the TMAs," says McDean. "And if Perseph can do what Kruse says it can do . . ."

Hopper laughs lowly. "Who the fuck knows. Goddamn, son . . . I know it's a video call, but every time that freaky queer speaks, I swear I smell the cum on his breath."

McDean scrupulously avoids commenting.

"Is he the boy or the girl, though?" muses Hopper aloud. "The fucker or the fuckee? Who's shooting whose wad in whose mouth, is what I guess I'm askin' he—"

To McDean's relief, there's a second *bloop!* and another monitor switches to a feed of a strangely ageless-looking man wearing a perfectly white suit, sitting in a perfectly black chair in a perfectly white room.

"Hallo?" says this new arrival. "John? John? Can you hear me correctly, please?"

McDean tries not to wince as he watches Hans-

Joachim Kruse speak. He's not sure what's worse to look at—Kruse's face or Hopper's body. Kruse is probably about the same age as Hopper, but he's subjected his body to so many radical treatments and surgeries and drugs that he no longer registers as fully human to McDean's eyes, so oddly pale and wet and gleaming and yet *stiff.* He's like a mannequin stuffed into a stitched-together sleeve of human skin, with a swatch of black-haired scalp delicately placed atop the skull.

"We can goddamn hear you, yes," says Hopper. "Didn't you design this shit? Doesn't it *always* work?"

Kruse blinks, unimpressed. The movement makes an unnerving *click* sound. "Hallo, Wayne," says Kruse. "John, hallo, hallo—how long do we have?"

"We've got a little over an hour until the peak window closes, Mr. Kruse," says McDean.

"What in hell does that mean, again?" says Hopper.

"It means our traffic forecasts show the number of people at the two remaining potential environments will peak in the next hour," says McDean. "After that, each environment offers diminishing returns. Our forecasts get more accurate the closer they get to the peak. We'll have about a fifteen-minute heads-up."

"Ain't these the same traffic models that said the rodeo would have three thousand fuckin' people?" asks Hopper.

"Ah," says McDean. "I'll have to check on that, sir."

"John," says Kruse. "I am showing that Perseph is fully loaded and ready for engagement, yes?"

"Correct, Mr. Kruse," says McDean.

"Excellent," says Kruse. "Good. Once activated, our data show it should create a *very* strong viewer affinity. Perfect for *Vigilance.*" He considers his phrasing, his thin lips (*very* thin lips) twitching. "Unless I am mistaken, it will cause actual, physical pain for viewers to look away once Perseph is engaged. What environment have you selected?"

"The mall, Mr. Kruse. At least, that's where things are trending."

Another blink, another awful *click.* "Good. Very good! Then we will have a baseline against which we can validate Perseph's performance, since you do malls so very often."

"It's *good* that we're goin' with another goddamn mall?" says Hopper, baffled.

"For the purposes of testing Perseph, yes," says Kruse. "We can compare target market activation levels to the last few mall events, and calibrate Perseph's affinities accordingly."

"I'm worried about damaging our relationship with our audience," says McDean. "Too many malls, and people won't be coming back."

"You do not understand, John," says Kruse. His German-accented English is as crisp and cold as a scalpel fresh from an alcohol wash. "With technology like Perseph, the content will no longer matter."

McDean tries to mask his discomfort. He's tried to articulate his concerns before, but Hans-Joachim Kruse is not a creature with any aptitude for concern. A former Silicon Valley titan, Kruse invested hugely in machine learning and neural networks when the technology was still in its nascent stages, and he is used to moving in bold, visionary strokes, sometimes describing his goals in quasi-religious tones, like he is the last surviving disciple of an order of priests.

McDean knows that the reality is different. Kruse is not as bloodless as he seems. The man's taken out entire legions of competitors either by burying them under lawsuits or hacking into them and destroying them from the inside. His flair for petty sadism is legendary: McDean's heard stories about Kruse's hack team driving a waiter to suicide just because the guy fucked up a *salad order.* Knowing that the man who funds most of ONT's technology also happens to have a voracious appetite for cruelty has a wearing effect on a man's mind.

Especially since Kruse's people developed this new tool—Perseph. McDean knows his own work's been revolutionary in his time at ONT: no one else has designed and placed advertising content better in the company's history, scientifically crafting signals and entertainment to assault the human brain. But he hadn't been aware that Kruse has been using his own processes and work to *teach* an AI.

Yet it makes sense—the more you can boil reality down to numbers and images, the easier it is for an AI to consume it, digest it, and learn from it.

And McDean's work, of course, is nothing but numbers and images.

He isn't sure what the entity known as Perseph does. No one did, really. No one knows how AIs work these days, except maybe the AIs that built them. But presumably, Perseph can do what McDean does, only better. *Far* better. And individualized, too: Perseph can learn who is watching their feeds, review what they like, and drop weaponized advertisements and copy right into the feeds, specifically designed to batter their thoughts—or that is the gist of it, at least.

From what Kruse has described, it isn't *quite* mind control. But it's close.

"Much of our research was inspired by gambling addicts," says Kruse. He licks his lips—his tongue, McDean notes, is a pale shade of yellow. "This expectation that if you just keep watching, keep refreshing, something wonderful will happen. It is this anticipation that Perseph has learned to capture, to stretch and distort beyond a second and into an hour, two hours, three, like a tantric practitioner prolonging an orgasm for half a day."

"That a fucked up way of sayin' sex sells?" asks Hopper.

"You will not want to activate Perseph until *Vigilance* has activated the peak number of visitors," says Kruse. "It can be a . . . disorienting thing to drop in on. They must be watching, and *then* it must be activated."

"It's still going to just look like regular television . . . right, Mr. Kruse?" asks McDean.

"Uhhh." Kruse has to think about it. "Quite possibly."

McDean considers his next comment. "Once Perseph has been given a successful test run . . . will I be able to view the research then?"

Kruse blinks once more, another horrid *click*—it sounds like someone smacking their lips, like his eyelids make suction. "Now, John," he says. "You know I cannot give you any insight into our research."

He sighs inwardly. "Yes, sir."

"Not without piling you under NDAs."

"Yes, sir."

"And unfortunately, all of the legal algos that manage ONT's contracts specifically forbid you from signing external NDAs."

"Didn't you design those, too?" says Hopper.

Kruse waves a hand dismissively. His wrist pokes out from his sleeve—it's as thin as a candlestick. "They were probably designed by another system. These things happen."

"Black boxes inside of black boxes," says McDean quietly.

"What was that?" asks Kruse.

"Nothing, Mr. Kruse." McDean's guts flutter unpleasantly. He does *not* want to piss off Kruse—but he can't share the man's blithe confidence when it comes to subjecting his entire audience to a subliminal AI about which he knows fucking nothing at all. He's heard Kruse's people conduct tests on prisoners, and the thought horrifies him: prisoners don't share the same race and economic backgrounds of any of his primary demographics at all. The population's all wrong! If that's his sample, then it's skewed, utterly fucked! This could *decimate* his TMAs.

His phone vibrates very softly in his pocket, and he freezes—McDean has taken great pains to make sure very, very few people know his contact information, and those who do have it know he doesn't want to be contacted *now,* of all times.

"Something wrong?" asks Hopper.

"My . . . phone, sir," says McDean.

Both men practice the same level of security when it comes to personal electronics—you don't touch them or tell anyone about them unless it's critical. "Something about the show?" asks Kruse.

"I don't know. I'll confirm, sir."

He takes out his phone, presses his fingertip into the

pad, lets the camera read his face, and breathes into the screen. (They need new biometrics every year to make these things more secure.)

When his phone unlocks, he's treated to the sight of a nude, twenty-one-year-old girl, sitting cross-legged on a hotel bed with half a cantaloupe positioned very strategically in her lap—its long, narrow seed core facing out, of course—as she carefully eats a half-peeled banana. She smiles impishly and winks for the camera.

McDean stares as the video loops over and over again. He blinks, feeling stunned, pleased, and a little outraged.

Goddamn it, Tabitha.

"John?" says Kruse. "Is everything all right?"

McDean swallows and puts his phone away. "Just confirmation that we're going with the mall," he says. "That's all, Mr. Kruse."

Hopper sits up, looking at something off-screen. "Oh, damn it, O'Donley's gone off the rails again."

"What?" says Kruse. "Who?"

"He's hollering like his ass is on fire," says Hopper. "McDean—when they gonna take that poor boy out back and shoot him?"

"When his ads peak," says McDean, relieved the subject has changed. Shawn O'Donley is ONT's biggest live pundit. His shows tend to get very loud and incoherent, and his viewers love it.

McDean shifts in his chair. He is painfully aware that he is now sporting a very decent erection. He is also aware that this very decent erection is surely very visible through his pants. And finally, he is also very, very, very aware that he is on a video call with his superiors, and that his superiors have the choice of viewing him from multiple angles.

"I'm afraid we've got to finalize our environment now," he says. "It looks like the mall's approaching peak optimization. Gentlemen, if there's nothing else . . ."

"Naw," says Hopper, sighing.

"No," says Kruse curtly.

"Then if you'll excuse me." He stands up. "I've got a show to start."

He turns and walks back out to the pits.

• • •

McDean walks out of the conference room and strides through his crew. He has to walk somewhat stiffly, since the tip of his erect penis is now carefully stuffed just below the waist of his pants.

"Numbers holding steady, chief," says Darrow as he passes.

"That's great," says McDean. He coughs. "Uh—so, any

of those numbers change?"

There's a pause.

"I . . . believe I just told you, boss, that they have not," says Darrow.

"Oh. Oh, right. And the peak traffic?"

"Peak will pass within forty-five minutes," says Darrow.

"Then fuck it," says McDean. "The mall's a go. Get our security units ready for the lockdown."

"Can do," says Darrow.

"I've got to make a goddamn call," says McDean.

"Uh," says Neal. "Okay, sir?"

McDean walks away, to a back hallway far removed from the control pits, toward an undistinguished black door. The door reads him—it's tuned for his biometrics—and it promptly unlocks. He slips inside, shuts it, and the lights flick on.

Inside is McDean's private bathroom—a very tasteful sink, stone sculpture, shower, and toilet.

He sets down his tablet, pulls out his phone, and unlocks it. Again, he's greeted by the sight of her gorgeous, perfectly symmetrical face, winking puckishly as she eats a banana.

God, that *wink*. It's got to be in the top ten of all-time winks, for sure.

He shakes his head, takes a breath, and calls her.

The phone rings once, twice. He finds he hopes she

doesn't answer.

Then there's a rustle, and her voice—high and gentle—chirrups, "Helllooooooo?"

"You ... You can't do that," he says, pacing in the bathroom.

"Can't do what? Say hello?"

"No. Send me stuff during the show."

"I can't send you stuff during the show?" she says coyly. "Or I can't send you *that* stuff during the show?"

"You can't send me stuff," he says, "and *especially* that stuff."

"I just wanted to give you something nice while you worked," she says, her voice dripping with faux offense. "And it *was* nice—wasn't it?"

McDean stops pacing. Then he says quietly, "Yes. Where are you?"

"I'm in my apartment, dumbass. Someone told me there's going to be a *Vigilance.* Don't you know you're not supposed to go outside when a *Vigilance* is going on?"

"Yeah. Yeah, I fucking heard."

"Did you. Do you miss me?"

He swallows. "Yes."

"It's been, what, two weeks? *God,* it takes a long time to do your show."

"It's all top secret. Nothing can get leaked out."

"Yeah, yeah, yeah, blah, blah, blah ... I was there during the intern training, you know. Hey—listen. A friend of mine from Princeton sent me this cool new app. Get this—it uses your phone's projector to send you a *live* 3-D video. Not a static one. Live. The person on the other end can show or do whatever you want."

"Yeah. Yeah, that sounds, uh, real cool."

A pause.

"I don't think you're getting what I'm saying," she says. "The person on the other end can *show* or *do* whatever you want."

He thinks about it, confused. "Oh. *Oh!*"

"Nowwww you get it. What if later, I show you all the things it can do?"

"Later during the show?"

"Like in a couple of hours or something, I guess."

"Tabitha . . ."

"What?"

"That's a bad idea."

"Why?" she asks. Again, the faux outrage.

"I can't download shit to my company phone."

"You've done it before."

"Yeah, but not while I was in here, during a *Vigilance*. All kinds of sensitive shit is going on."

"Suit yourself. But I just want to let you know, I finally figured out this one stretch in yoga that I've been working on for for*ever*, and I did want to show it to you. It's this thing where I can put my whole neck against the floor, and flip my hips up and over . . ."

He swallows. "Oh, God."

She laughs—a high, tinkly, champagne sound. "I take it that's a yes?"

"Ohhh . . . Fine," he says. "Yes, goddamn it, that's . . . that's a yes."

"Good. Call you later?"

"Yes," he says.

"Okay. You take care of yourself, okay, John?"

"I will."

She laughs, and the phone goes dead.

McDean stands there in his bathroom, staring at his darkened phone.

What a fucking moron he is. What a fool he is—he, John McDean, Director of Entertainment and Marketing, Master of the Universe—to get so tied in knots over a girl. A *girl*.

But he can't help himself. He unlocks his phone again and watches the looped video of her on the bed, his eyes fixed on her face.

Tabitha is McDean's latest acquisition, bagged at the start of intern season when the colleges started rotating in new flesh. Intern season is a prized ONT tradition, because interns are the only females you ever really see on the production side: when you have software that can generate any image of any woman, employing actual female news anchors isn't necessary.

Tabitha, though . . . She wasn't just some intern. That girl was a thoroughbred, belonging to that special breed of human being whose sheer attractiveness would give anyone pause. She was, as Perry put it, "the shiniest goddamn penny in the piggy bank"—and when she walked in, she seemed to just know that such interns were reserved for John McDean, Master of the Fucking Universe.

It's only been going on for a couple of months. Yet McDean's desire for her has been insatiable: he wants to take her, to hold her, to feel every part of her, to consume her. His obsession almost borders on the vampiric.

Of course, all the interns get booted out during the windup to *Vigilance*. *Vigilance* is way too confidential to allow a bunch of college girls wandering through the halls, including Tabitha.

But he . . . does miss her. He *thinks*. Maybe that's what this feeling is. Since he studies biological reaction to stimuli for a living, he is keenly aware of his raised heart rate, the horripilation of his skin, the prickling of sweat on his temples, and, last but not least, the continuing turgidity in his pants.

He is not sure why he's so magnetically drawn to her. Perhaps this is all just a hoary cliché, and he's trying to recapture lost youth. Like most moderately wealthy Americans, McDean never really had one. Going to school in America in the '20s started to feel like going to school in an airport, all checkpoints and X-rays and bullet-proof backpacks and armed guards. And it's pretty fucking hard to get laid in an airport.

He knows he had it good, though. The country had become an unforgiving place to be a child by then. His schools had guards. Others hadn't.

But he sometimes imagines—what would that have been like, to just . . . be? To be a kid and not think about the increasingly high odds of being murdered, or dying in some ecological catastrophe? To play, and grow, and learn, and love? Unblemished and whole.

He likes to imagine he beholds such a phenomenon in Tabitha. A bright, springy, contented creature, unburdened by the world. To see her smile, to clutch her soft shoulders . . . God. He knows he won't ever have a child of his own—only a fucking moron or someone preposterously wealthy would bring a kid into this dying, smoking world—but he still has a raw, teeming hunger to know youth, to see innocence, to hold his palms out to it like it's a glimmering fire and witness it before it sputters out, probably forever.

John McDean looks at her face for a minute longer. Then his tablet blinks on—an alert.

He glances at it—peak traffic is approaching.

"Fuck," he says. He grabs his tablet and storms out of the bathroom.

• • •

The tenor of chatter in the pits has grown considerably now. It's like delivering a baby—everyone knows it's close.

McDean looks at his tablet and runs his own models, integrating the environment and traffic-flow data with his own marketing algorithms, trying to time everything *perfectly.*

He runs the analysis, reviews the numbers. He walks to the center of the pits and holds up his hand.

The production room falls silent. They all watch him, like he's returned from some foreign battle with grave news.

He looks up. "Nine twenty-three," he says loudly. "Our drop time is *nine twenty-three.* What is our fucking drop time, gentlemen?"

"*Nine twenty-three!*" they shout back in unison.

"Nine twenty-three. Perry!"

"Yessir," says Perry from the sitter pit.

"Enviro crossover with our actives?"

"Three candidates," says Perry. "All with solid relation scores."

"Bonnan included?"

Perry stuffs another wad of chaw in his mouth and shakes his head. "No records of him visiting the environment."

"Boot the weakest and throw Bonnan in. I've got a liking for that kid. In twenty minutes, have the shuttles converge on the environment and let the actives pick their gear."

"You got it, hoss," says Perry.

"Ives?" calls McDean.

"Yes, sir," says Ives, blinking sleepily.

"Spin 'em up," says McDean. "Get your brand influencers started on putting out the word. I want rumors that a *Vigilance* is about to drop at any moment with *extra* focus on the mid-Atlantic seaboard."

"Starting up the chorus," says Ives.

"Calibrate your bots for aggression," says McDean. "I want fights. I want people bitching and clawing at people about when the next *Vigilance* starts, about who'd survive and who'd turn puss. I want people talking about *nothing* but *Vigilance.*"

"I've made sure to stuff a lot of the main trends," says Ives. "We'll suck all the blood out of them ASAP, draw the convos away."

"Good," says McDean. "Darrow, Neal—do we have an external array?"

"Got about forty hacked security cameras on the outside of the mall," says Darrow. "Good angles. I've woken the drones, they'll be filtering throughout the mall shortly."

"Excellent." They'd once had a whole pit just for drone pilots, but the AIs have gotten smart enough by now that they do almost everything for you. "Throw up the main feed on the big screen."

The room hears him, and a huge, gleaming, razor-thin black surface slowly drops from the far wall. There's a click, and it turns into a giant, glowing video screen.

On the screen is a big, beefy man in a tight suit with slicked-back, graying hair. He's seated at a news desk, holding a cooked, glistening rib-eye steak in each hand, and he appears to be screaming at the top of his lungs. At the bottom of this is the chyron: TAKING OUR MEAT AWAY??

"Shit," says Perry. "The hell is O'Donley up to now?"

"Give me some volume," says McDean.

The monitor hears him, and turns it up.

". . . *going to say what we can eat, what we can do?*" he bellows. "*We are LOSING the fight, people! We are under SIEGE! Our way of life is being LOST to these discontented agitators! And I, for one, WILL. NOT. HAVE IT!*" The man takes a giant bite out of one rib eye, then the other, his face glistening with hot grease.

"Jesus Christ," says Neal quietly.

"*This is what a real man looks like!*" screams Shawn O'Donley. Still clutching the steaks, he points at his full mouth with both index fingers. "*This is a tough boy you're gonna have to get some dyno-mite—some TEE-IN-TEE—to dislodge from this chair! Ka-POW!*" He throws the steaks at the camera, then stoops under his desk. He resurfaces with an armful of pristine leather footballs. "*Bam! Bam! Bam!*" he screams, hurling the footballs at someone just off-screen.

McDean has to give the man some credit—the spirals are tight, and the passes are near perfect. But they would be. O'Donley was a tight end at Michigan, and he even played in the Senior Bowl, though he didn't get drafted. McDean is fairly sure that O'Donley's thick, square, Irish-ass head has taken so many blows that his brain must be riddled with chronic traumatic encephalopathy, just a loose gob of pudding swirling around in his skull. None of this has impacted the view ratings on *The O'Donley Effect*, however: though the man's behavior has steadily degraded to the point where every show has a lot of screaming, stomping around, and, more and more frequently, taking his shirt off, the audience—and especially McDean's Ideal Person—absolutely loves him.

They don't know that after the show, O'Donley wanders the halls of ONT like a lost, confused child, struggling with door handles. They don't know how he stares around, bewildered, his tiny eyes glistening with tears, the brittle, blinking gaze of a sentimental drunk.

McDean gives him a year until he's rotting in the ground. But ONT's captured a lot of video of him, and he's got a pretty standard shtick. It shouldn't be too hard to generate new episodes. Besides, this is great for numbers.

"We'll be coasting off of O'Donley, right into *Vigilance*," McDean says. "Perfect." He looks at Andrews. "We've got our faces and pipes together?"

"Compiling now," says Andrews. "I'll have our on-air talent generated shortly."

"And we've all got our on-air scripts filled, yes?" shouts McDean to the control room.

"Yes," they all say back.

"You better," says McDean. "I don't want our anchor saying some dumbass word salad tonight."

He looks at his tablet, checks the numbers. It's just been minutes, but Ives has already goosed all his social media resources—traffic on the feeds has quintupled.

Everyone knows there's a *Vigilance* coming. They've been waiting for it. Everyone *needs* to see a *Vigilance*.

He watches the numbers build and build. The control room thrums with chatter as people race from pit to pit, comparing numbers, data, info. The main feed's muted itself again. O'Donley is gripping an American flag in one hand, his fingers shiny with beef fat, and is pointing at a projected image of Lady Bird Johnson with the other and screaming.

McDean keeps watching the metrics: the page views, the mentions, how many cumulative viewers they're building, which advertisements are getting the most traffic on the disparate ONT platforms.

"Security's in place," says Darrow.

"And our actives are two minutes out," drawls Perry.

"Drones ready to filter in," says Neal.

McDean checks the time. Nine ten. Time to pull it.

He looks at Andrews and nods. "Launch."

Andrew runs the script, and O'Donley fades out, and the show begins.

"It's happening!" cries a man from a booth. "It's happening!"

Delyna looks up from her meditations. She'd intentionally put her phone away—she hadn't wanted to actually see it coming, to feel its approach—yet now it seems to be here.

The man from the booth—the guy in the Oklahoma hat—charges over to the bar. "Change the channel!" he says excitedly. He points a finger at one of the screens, which are currently showing a basketball game. "Change the channel!"

Delyna narrows her eyes at him. It was not a request, she notices, but a command.

"Come on, come on, come on!" he says.

You've been coming here for over a year, she thinks, *but all you ever give me is orders.*

She reluctantly picks up the remote control and changes the channel to ONT. She's dreading the sights, the sounds—but it seems it's not here yet, if it's really coming: right now the channel shows another episode of that screaming guy, the one who'd been saying lesbians were infiltrating America's utilities sector.

But then the credits roll . . . and the screen darkens.

Why am I still here? she thinks miserably.

The dreadful hum fills the South Tavern. The patrons stand and gather before the screens, whooping and chattering and quivering like religious zealots at a sermon.

Why didn't I leave this awful place? Why did I stay here?

McDean watches, barely breathing.

The screen is black, accompanied by a low hum. (They have developed this hum to the point of perfection, a frequency sampled from earthquakes in Japan—the noise instantly triggers anxiety in some primal annex of the human mind.)

Then the screen abruptly changes to black-and-white newsfeed of riots, seething crowds of filthy protestors pouring down the street, throwing bottles, cans, rocks.

A husky, smoky, masculine voice says, *"Are you prepared?"*

A montage of pundits and chyrons and headlines: TERRORISM ON THE RISE? followed by COLLAPSE OF LAW AND ORDER and CRIME RATE SKYROCKETS.

Then a blur of worried white faces, one after the other, their sentences layered on top of one another: *"... threatening all inside ..."* and *"... possible for a civilization to even sustain itself?"* and finally, a sober old man saying, *"... without a doubt, our future is absolutely, totally, completely in jeopardy."*

McDean checks the numbers, the feeds, the hits, the

mentions: they've octupled, nontupled, near-exponential growth, a rapid blur of panic out there in the heartland.

He sees the main trends, with one word predominant: *Where?*

Where's it going to happen? Who's going to get it? Who's ready?

God, I love this, he thinks, his pulse pounding. *God, God, God, I love this.*

Again, the voice says, "*Are you prepared?*"

Night vision video of some nondescript Middle Easterners swarming an embassy, AK-47s chattering and popping. Drone footage of missile sites being bombed.

Tattered little boats pouring into harbors, piled high with desperate refugees. Filthy shantytowns full of hollow-eyed brown children. A desert encampment on fire.

The voice says, "*Are you alert?*"

Another montage of respectable, concerned-looking pundits (McDean can't remember if any of these people or stories are real or generated, though he knows it honestly doesn't matter) saying, "*. . . we simply aren't focusing enough on our law enforcement and our defense strategies . . .*" followed by "*. . . the bad guys are* ahead *of us. They're slipping through our filters, our screens!*" and then, "*. . . technology is not dependable. It can be compromised. Everything can be compromised . . .*"

The montage ends in a clip of the man himself, Shawn

O'Donley, saying, "*The true fight will not come from some branch of the military, or the government, or law enforcement. The true fight, the strongest defense, will come from us. From us. From patriots, from the foresighted and the true of heart, who can see the threat—and have the bravery to meet it.*"

It gives McDean goosebumps every time. O'Donley, of course, hasn't been that articulate or composed in years, but Andrews is just a fucking wizard, and he made that clip happen in less than two days.

The voice fills the room, thundering, "*Are you VIGI-LANT?*"

Dramatic music floods the room—drums, French horns, noble but troubled. The screen changes to a slick, brightly lit studio, glowing with reds and blues, and a huge desk. Behind the desk sits a woman with bright blond hair, ruby lips, and a solid blue dress (Pantone 653). The voice says, "*Live, from ONT studios . . . we bring you tonight's* Vigilance*!*"

"Adjust your scripts if you need to, gents," says McDean. "But only slightly. It's balls-to-the-wall time now."

Almost instantly, a betting pool emerges from the commotion in the South Tavern. The man in the Oklahoma hat is the one leading the charge, wheeling through the small throng of people and saying, " . . . can't get any traction in Vegas, not from here. But if you want in, now's your chance, okay?"

Delyna watches them, bewildered by this eruption of rituals. They bet on the environment selection, then start formulating how they'll bet on the shooters. Then her phone vibrates—it's the bar owner, Martin.

She picks it up, and she hears his voice: "Hey, I was gonna come in, but I'm trapped where I am. You got people trapped at the bar, yeah?"

"Yes," says Delyna. She knows what he's going to say.

"Excellent. Put on happy hour prices for drinks and appetizers. And can you stay late tonight? You never know how long these things can last. Once they had a fuckin' siege, went for hours. *Hours,* Darla!"

She sighs inwardly. She knows she can stay late tonight. "Yes, sir," she says.

"Great. And hey—you stay safe, okay, Darla?"

"Yes, sir," she says. She doesn't bother correcting his mistake. He gets irritated when she does it, and she can't afford to lose shifts or her job.

He hangs up. She turns to Raphael and says, "Get your shit ready. Happy hour pricing."

He laughs. "God damn. Gotta make a buck, huh?"

"I guess." Delyna picks up a chalkboard, scrawls out HAPPY HOUR UNTIL VIGILANCE ENDS, and slams it on the bar top loud enough for everyone to hear.

The small crowd turns, sees the board, and claps. Then they pivot back to the show.

McDean watches closely as it begins. The camera closes in on the woman at the desk—she's reading papers, actual paper. Nobody does that shit anymore, but their audience loves it. They think it makes her look intellectual.

The woman stares into the camera. Her face is serious, but her eyes are alight with excitement. "Good evening, ladies and gentlemen," she says. "I'm Stacey Robwright." Robwright is, of course, the sort of high-powered, conservative, cosmopolitan lady that John McDean's Ideal Person absolutely adores. "Tonight, America's mettle, its resilience, and its fortitude will be tested yet again in *Vigilance*. Will American civilians be up to the challenge? Will they be ready to face the many threats that have invaded our nation? Can they prove themselves to be the defense force we desperately need for our culture, our heritage, and our way of life to survive this day and age? We'll find out soon enough."

McDean watches Robwright's face carefully. The spacing between her eyes, the shading on her cheeks, the way her hair falls across her brow. Then he chides himself for bothering—Andrews has poisoned his brain. She looks fine. She looks *great*.

"Joining me is Bob Bowder," she says, "who's on the ground at the city where our next *Vigilance* will take place, but the specific environment has yet to be revealed. Bob, what can you tell us?"

The feed changes to a white man of about thirty, with dark hair and handsome features. He looks like a former shortstop or tennis player, a slick, talented guy who knows exactly how talented he was. There's always a ghost of a smirk around his mouth, like he's imagining how easy it'd be to fuck your wife. "Good evening, Stacey, great to be with you here for another *Vigilance*. I'm here in Daileyton, Indiana, just outside of Fort Wayne—and Daileyton is the town that will be tested before the watching world. Our three potential *Vigilance* sites tonight are an ice rink, a mall, and a train station. Let's learn about them."

"Looks good?" asks Andrews in the control room.

"Yeah," says McDean. "Yeah, looks good."

All of it, of course, is bullshit. ONT does not employ two individuals with the names of Stacey Robwright or Bob Bowder. It does not own a garishly lit, red-and-blue studio. The only thing ONT sent to Daileyton, Indiana, was a shitload of money to pay the contractors that make up their handler and security teams.

All of this—*all* of it—is generated. The images of Bowder and Robwright are drawn from actors hired to walk around, talking and moving in certain fashions over a couple of weeks (McDean knows this, because he fucked the girl who created Robwright's base movements, in his private bathroom), but otherwise, it's a show of ghosts, just shadow play and noise. Bowder, Robwright, and all the other "experts" that the audience watches are programs that Andrews and other coders have created.

McDean's people manage the raw data, the lines, and the scripts. They call it the "faces and pipes" aspect of production, just voices and visages. About half of it is literally drag-and-drop: write a sentence or a fact, drag it, and drop it into the AIs' feeds. Computers make the rest: the images, the sounds, everything, all calculated to appeal to the marketing analytics they develop every nanosecond of every day.

The show moves on. Bowder narrates a few feeds of security cameras and hacked drone videos from the three potential environments—this video, of course, is supplied by Neal and Darrow. It's all very, very well done.

"The question," Bowder gravely intones, "is: have these people *prepared* themselves?"

The skating rink and the train stations aren't potentials anymore, of course—the mall is *the* place. It's set in stone now. None of these feeds are live now, either—this is footage from two to three hours ago. Right now, the rink and train station have probably erupted into a panic as people hear that they might be the site of a *Vigilance.*

But the mall continues as normal. Darrow and Neal are very, very good at limiting communication in or out of a chosen space. And besides, the actives will be introduced soon.

McDean passes by Perry's pit and watches as the software scans his input, isolating key phrases and numbers in seconds. Perry idly watches the program mine away, absently spitting chaw spit into his giant plastic cup.

"We now go to Jessie Gramins, who's here to tell us about tonight's contestants," says the collection of pixels and soundbites that claims to be Stacey Robwright.

"Thanks, Stacey." Jessie is generated to be an older black man, serious and thoughtful, like a law professor. (McDean knows his target audience can only tolerate black men over a certain age. If they skew too young, his audience will categorize them as a threat—even if they don't know it—and that can hurt their TMAs.) "We've got three contestants in tonight's Daileyton *Vigilance.* The first is Conor Stewart, age twenty-three, from Kokomo." The kid's mug shot pops up in the corner. He looks skinny, resentful—perfect. "We've got the classic signs here: a dropout, troubled family, inability to connect with others, and—perhaps the most classic sign here—a disrespect for his national legacy. Here's an essay that Stewart wrote in high school, questioning the ability of America's armed forces to seal the deal and bring home victory abroad."

Images of the text flash up on the screen. On split screen, Stacey Robwright shakes her head, looking shaken. "Sad."

"Isn't it?" says Gramins. "Isn't it?"

"That's not what the boys on the front lines want to hear at all, no," says Robwright.

"Nice," McDean says to Perry. "Very nice."

"Thanks, hoss." He spits chaw into the cup. "Thought you'd like it."

"Next up is Michael Rison," says Gramins, "and this is a very striking story: his father lost his job at the lumber mill six years ago, after the mill closed down due to unfair competition from abroad." His photo shows a thick, small-eyed, sullen boy with a scrubby patch of chin hair. "Rison fell into crime and drugs after this—I'm told he harbors a lot of anger."

"Well, I would too," says Robwright, feigning outrage. "It just makes me wonder—when are we going to do something, anything, about China?"

"Maybe tonight will change America's mind," says Gramins. "Time will tell, Stacey."

This talking point is automatically drawn from the trending topics on ONT's platforms. China is a constant draw—ONT's viewers have always dreaded and hated it, even before it surpassed America in . . . well. Everything.

"And our third and final contestant is Gabriel Bonnan, a transplant from Iowa, where as you know, Stacey, the state is involved in a thoughtful, ongoing debate about heritage and patriotism—and Bonnan was on the front lines." They show an image of Gabriel Bonnan in a suit and tie, his hair expertly parted, his tie expertly tied, standing in a line of well-muscled, white, dapper-looking young Nazis. It is incredibly, incredibly real-looking.

"Holy shit!" says McDean. "Andrews, Jesus . . . Wow!"

"You're welcome," says Andrews.

McDean tamps down his astonishment, and reconsiders this. "I guess we're going with the nice spin on Bonnan?"

"The audience we've pulled . . . they love them some white boys, that's for sure," says Perry.

"Even if they're fucking Nazis?"

"Hey, man," says Perry. "White is white."

It never fails to amuse McDean: his target demographic, his Ideal Person, absolutely worships the Second World War—and yet, when it comes to genuine, actual Nazis at home, they curiously don't mind so much.

"Bonnan fell out of the Iowan civil rights movement

after it was infiltrated by bad actors," continues Gramins on the screen. "And, like many youths in America, he was lured away by urban drugs, and their sex gangs."

"Aw, we gotta work on *that* shit," says McDean. "'*Sex gangs*'? How the fuck is *that* in the algos' vocab?"

"It's being pulled from newspaper reports," says Andrews. "Apparently, local news in Indiana is pretty terrible."

"Let's try and get some better filters put together, please?" says McDean. "Indiana local news might be shit, but I don't want their dumbass turns of phrase filtering back into *Vigilance*."

On the screen, Stacey Robwright sits up, listening. "I'm . . . I'm being told that, yes, *Vigilance* is indeed very close . . . As always, we do not yet know the location of tonight's *Vigilance,* but the three active shooters are ready to pick their arsenal as they prepare to assault the moral fabric of this nation."

"Cycle it up," says McDean to Ives. "Start pummeling similar locations with ads—other train stations, sporting event sites, other malls."

"Already on it," says Ives. Shortly, McDean knows, countless mall shoppers in America will glance at their social media feeds and see sponsored ads of a mall just like the one they're in *right now*—only, that one might be the site of a *Vigilance*. Mothers and fathers and brothers and sisters will tune in, see security feeds of families just like their own—people just like them—and wonder: *Are they gonna make it? Are they vigilant enough? Am I vigilant enough?*

The main ONT feed cuts to overhead feeds of the active shooters—Stewart, Rison, and Bonnan. They huddle in the handlers' shuttles, reviewing the gear in the box before them. Each piece of gear is held behind a little glass shutter: once they exceed their points, all the shutters lock. McDean's always worried that they're going to pick a grenade, pull the pin, and blow up the handler's shuttle right then and there—but their marketing research has done its job. Every time, they pick people who genuinely, really want to carry out a mass shooting.

Stewart proves to be a dumbass. He picks the body armor, a Klimke 78 pistol, and an extended clip, using up all of his one thousand points. This is the stupidest possible approach—the armor is unwieldy if you're not used to it, slowing you down, and a pistol takes actual marksmanship to use. Unless he had police training—and McDean knows he fucking didn't—he'll be slow and ineffectual.

Rison is somewhat smarter. He chooses a pistol, two grenades, and a better entrance. However, grenades are not as stupid-proof as people think. They take training, and McDean has seen lots of *Vigilance* competitors accidentally blow themselves up. Lots.

This choice provokes indignant scoffs in the control room. "What's with these dumbasses trying to mix it up?" says Darrow. "Are they working from a spreadsheet or something?"

"I told you," says Perry. "These boys are too stupid to put on their own goddamn pants."

But Bonnan . . . Bonnan goes for the classic: the AL-18 assault rifle, with an extended clip and a stim. A whole lot of firepower at an obscene rate, and your blood running hot with amphetamines and God knows what else.

"Running some social media polls," says Ives. "People are already voting like nuts, speculating who's going to win. The guy with the grenades is ahead—they like that 'shock-and-awe' shit. The betting markets in Las Vegas have picked up instantly. Narrative's coming in well, generating .86 on the engagement scale."

"And the number of interactions?" asks McDean.

Ives whistles. "We're breaking numbers, chief," he says. "Over two million in thirty seconds."

McDean takes a slow breath. That's exactly what he wanted to hear—and they haven't even revealed the environment yet.

The show pulls in some pundits who analyze the shooters' choices, discussing what sort of urban environments their weapons would be ripe for. "This is exactly what we saw in the house-to-house warfare in Canada," says a man in military fatigues. "I don't know if Rison is taking tips from soldiers—but I'd say he's definitely got a very aggressive, very urban-oriented strategy in mind, very shock-and-awe."

Time for the ad break, right before they open the doors and all hell breaks loose.

"We'll be right back," says Stacey Robwright, smiling triumphantly.

. . .

The ads flicker by, one after the other, timed perfectly. McDean's eyes trace them like a general watching cavalry units cross a battlefield.

Soft-cover toilet seats. Armor-piercing rounds. Catheter delivery services. Security cameras. Car cameras, for the internal and external. Walkers. Editions of the Holy Bible. Limited edition plates commemorating the latest American disaster. Drugs. Drugs. Medical services. Comfort robots. Some more drugs.

On and on and on.

He drinks them in, watching the tiny gestures, the little, special moments that he knows will anchor each ad in the right demographic's mind. One ad shows a virile, muscular white man, wearing jeans and no shirt, standing on his farmhouse porch with a pistol in his hand. There's a close-up of the pistol—his wrists thick and veined and meaty and rippling, excellently subliminal stuff. Holding the gun, he looks amplified, magnified, just *bigger*. His wife is beside him, small and delicate in her gauzy nightgown—she's a pixie, fragile as a leaf. The man, it appears, is defending his home from invaders, who are a spectrum of minorities—Hispanic, black, Asian, one of them might be a Pacific Islander, it depends on the algo—though they all wear do-rags, and baggy shirts, and ridiculous pants. Exactly what these distinctly urban characters are doing attacking this guy's fucking farm in the middle of the night is unclear—are they going to steal his horses, or his goddamn corn?—nor is it clear why his wife has chosen to join him, exposing herself to danger in her bright, white nightgown. And why are they well lit, while the attackers are in the dark? McDean knows none of this matters—not to the audience.

The powerful man fires away at the assailants, taking down one, two, three bad guys. The rest turn and flee, the ends of their do-rags whipping in the wind. As the woman clutches the man's meaty torso, the logo of the sports equipment retailer splashes up on the screen, along with a URL and a slogan: FOR YOUR HOME, FOR THE FIELD, FOR AMERICA.

"Numbers!" shouts McDean.

"Sixty-four," says Ives.

His eyebrows crawl up his brow. They're *starting* with a .64 on their target market activation ratios? That's fucking unbelievable!

Another ad, this one for a tax service for people deep in medical debt—which is most of *Vigilance*'s core audience, of course. Images of wholesome, white professionals parade across the screen, accompanied by flashing red words like PROTECT YOURSELF FROM FRAUD! Of course, no financial work is being done by such men—it's all computers these days, and the computers whose services are being sold in these ads aren't nearly as smart as the computers that conspired to put the target audience into debt in the first place.

McDean watches as the screen flashes WATCH OUT! and BEWARE! This one is a little over the top, but all of his ads are generated to maximize anxiety, which is exactly what he wants.

Another ad—this one is for a "tactical light." McDean personally has no fucking clue what a tactical light is—how can a light be tactical?—but the ad shows another beefy, military-looking dude, clad in camo, sporting a serious look and a serious crew cut. He is walking across his driveway to go get his newspaper (another anachronism the audience expects and loves) when he hears a *snap* sound from behind. He whirls, whips his hand out, and turns on his tactical light, which flashes a bright spotlight on . . . his young son, wearing feetsie pajamas (patterned in ducks and balloons) and clutching his blanket (Pantone 304). *"Sorry, Daddy,"* he says. *"I just wanted to see you some more before you go fight for our country again."* The beefy dude's serious glower dissolves into a pleasant smile, and he walks over and picks up his son. *"I'm home now, though,"* he says. He looks into the camera and says, *"And home is* safe." Then he turns on his tactical light, hands it to his son, and lets him light the way as they walk back into the house. Then the logo flashes on the screen.

"Andrews, did you see the problem there?" says McDean.

Andrews sighs. "He didn't go pick up the paper."

"No," says McDean. "He went out to go get the newspaper, and yet he left it there."

"Maybe he forgot it?" says Ives.

"Maybe his son is more important than the paper?" proposes Neal.

"It's not that," says McDean. "It's an AI fuckup. Something to fix in the future."

Another ad, then another—and then it's back to *Vigilance.* It's time to start the show.

• • •

Stacey Robwright holds a hand to her ear, pretending to listen. "I'm . . . I'm being told that tonight's *Vigilance* could be . . . yes, it's now imminent. We'll know shortly which of the three sites has been chosen."

Cut to feeds of the three actives in their shuttles—each feed has STEWART, RISON, or BONNAN in the corner.

"Let's confirm that our bodycams are active," says Robwright, "to make sure we can understand what's happening from the perspective of the threat."

"And, Stacey," says some vaguely military-looking pundit, "this is honestly *so* important for the public, to see what the perpetrator is thinking, what they're doing, what their goals are."

McDean paces in the control room and asks, "Perry?"

"All set," says Perry.

The feed cycles though the bodycam feeds, these also stamped with STEWART, RISON, BONNAN. They're also suited up with a neat little shoulder bodycam that can show the shooter's face and expressions.

"We can see them," says Robwright on the screen. "So we can understand them . . . Yes."

"I do not want to hear any more of this fucking philosophizing," says McDean.

"Got it," says Andrews from the back.

"Her mouth looks *great,* though, Andrews," he says.

Andrews scowls.

"All right," says Robwright on the screen. "And now . . . Yes, they're in position."

Feeds of the three shooters huddled before the shuttle doors. The main feed then splits into three different subscreens, showing the shooters' perspectives as they wait, all rattling, blurry videos from their bodycams.

"This is so intense, Stacey," says Bowder. "This is always such an intense experience. Who's going to make it? Who isn't?"

"This is a true, honest-to-God—I apologize for my offensive language, but that's truly how I feel about it—an honest-to-God test of America," says Robwright. "And now . . ."

The shuttle doors fly open.

Stewart, Rison, and Bonnan leap out of the shuttles and find themselves faced with glass doors—through which you can see the busy walkways of the mall.

"It looks like . . . yes, it looks like the mall!" says Robwright. "Is it the mall?"

"It's the *mall*, Stacey," says Gramins.

"Oh my God, it is," says Bowder, sounding excited and horrified. "It's the mall. And *Vigilance* begins!"

In the control room, McDean whirls to snarl at Andrews. "Robwright's supposed to say that," he snaps. "Not fucking Bowder."

"I thought it'd be interesting to mix it up," says Andrews.

"Well, it isn't. We need to maintain our branding."

The shooting begins.

. . .

It's not pretty, coordinated, or easy to follow—but then, it never is, and McDean's team is very used to that.

The main feed is still split into three different sub-screens. In one, Stewart opens the door, staggers through, raises his pistol, and starts firing indiscriminately at the crowd. In a second, Rison walks through and starts fumbling with a grenade—his hands are shaking. A lot. In the third, Bonnan walks through the doors, lifts his AL-18, draws a careful bead on a man staring at his phone while holding his wife's bag, and opens fire.

"Pivoting to angle shots," says Neal.

The three windows move to drone footage. The drones are smaller than the palm of your hand, possess cameras more advanced than a Hollywood blockbuster's, and have been imprinted on the three active shooters: they follow them like a play camera might in the NFL, zipping behind the main actors. Most of the drones are keyed into the movements of the shooter's gun—they line up so you can *kind* of see what they're shooting at. This is critical, because mass shootings are, like most shootings, confusing and difficult to understand. It's not like a sport where you can see where the ball is, where it's going, who it's intended for, and who wants to take the ball away from them. It's just a wild blur.

Bonnan's shot is true: the man holding his wife's bag drops to the ground, eyes staring up in dull surprise. Stewart hits, like, fucking nobody—he catches some white lady in the leg, and a glass wall of a shop explodes behind her, but for the most part, his shots are all over the place. Rison, wisely, has chosen a deserted entrance close to the stairs: he quickly makes for the stairway and runs up, hoping to get a better angle on the action, maybe heading for the food court.

"This is always what shakes me the most," says Robwright's voice darkly on the screen. "How un-alert these people are. They are just not paying attention. They just are *not*."

Bonnan has switched to full auto now and is just shredding people: an old Asian man in a parka slumps over, blood pouring from his skull; his wife spins around like she's forgotten something, but she's missing most of her lower arm; a family of six—chunky white people in sweats—are sitting on a bench, looking at their phones, and they don't even see the gun before the hail of bullets plows into their torsos, legs, faces, and they wilt like plants in desert heat. A girl of about seven is screaming by a stone water fountain—then the fountain erupts in dust as the bullets saw into it. When the dust clears, she's lying facedown with her arm at a strange angle.

"Bonnan is taking a classic approach here," says some army guy in military fatigues in a sub-screen window. "He's taking full advantage of these people's state of complacency."

McDean steps closer to the screen. "It's getting hard to keep track of these quasi-army fucks," he says. "Let's winnow them down, please."

"Got it," says Andrews.

"Just taking maximal advantage of these citizens," continues Army Man. "They're just not ready, and he's got a high-velocity weapon with a high firing rate. Unless you're prepared, what you're seeing could happen to you."

"I just don't understand," says Robwright. "How can these people let this happen to their families? How can they not be *ready*?"

"I just don't know, Stacey," says Gramins. "I really just don't know."

Another burst of gunfire rings through the control room.

Delyna is filling up yet another pitcher of beer when she hears the sound: the chatter and tinny crack of gunfire, the eruption of screams.

The surface of the beer in the pitcher quivers: her hands are shaking. She doesn't want to look, doesn't want to see it, but she can't help it. She glances up and spies the three strangely fish-eyed feeds capturing the pandemonium and terror, just three boxes on the screens, each with an arm holding a pistol emerging from the bottom left corner—or, in one instance, some kind of much larger assault rifle. In two of the screens, the gun is shooting. The third is not—not yet, at least.

The crowd at the South Tavern whoops and claps like spectators at a horse race. It seems some of them bet on the mall being the selection, and they've made a good bit of money with their guess. Those who bet against them appear only mildly downcast. It is hard, it seems, to feel bad when you are witnessing such grand entertainment.

Delyna finishes putting another tray together, then scoops up two orders of cheese fries from Raphael's order counter. She waits on the last element—chips and salsa—and stares back at the crowd.

These people. They are much like her, working-class and only somewhat educated, but they seem to be from some other nation, where guns and violence are a cheerful fantasy and not a reality as it had been for Delyna. It comes down to entitlement, she supposes: the people in the South Tavern grew up being told that, if a shooting happened, then they would be the survivors, the ones shooting back, or the ones righteously doing that shooting in the first place. The world had not told Delyna or people like her any such thing. Perhaps her role in the frenetic narrative these people dream of is simply that of a victim: sad, perfunctory, but necessary for the story to work.

Or perhaps she's been forgotten altogether. She is not the intended audience for this story. That has always been clear.

Raphael slides over a basket of chips and salsa. She picks it up and drops the order off at the tables around the televisions. No one seems to notice.

Again, she thinks, *Why am I still here? Why didn't I leave with everyone else?*

The question plagues her more and more. She's seen posts from her departed friends on Nuuvu depicting their happy, contented new lives in South America, or China, or Africa, or Europe. The world is turbulent and changing, that is clear—Europe is still recovering from the last hurricane—but at least in those places, it isn't actively hostile.

But she knows why she hasn't left: because she believed that things would change. That they would get better. She wasn't sure why—she just thought it would. Such an idea had been engraved in her mind since childhood: the arc of the moral universe is long, but it bends toward justice. It is the American story, or so she thought.

Yet she's realized all too late that it is exactly that—a story. An idea, a fiction, or maybe even a piece of propaganda designed to keep her here and quiet. Perhaps change isn't always slow and incrementally positive. Perhaps it can be fast, and for the worse.

Perhaps things will never get better. Perhaps the present is also the future.

Delyna listens to the gunfire in her ears and pours another beer.

McDean stands stock-still in the control room, watching. In the STEWART window, people are scrambling like crazy. One civilian has produced a pistol, and is about to shoot back at Stewart—the drones' AIs recognize the gun and zero in on it, highlighting the story.

"This man, though—is he ready? Is he *trained*?" says Robwright.

The man—he looks like a little league coach—hesitates before he fires at Stewart. He blinks as the gun goes off, and his aim, like Stewart's, is terrible. Stewart is all keyed up now, though, feeling the groove, and he takes cover behind a column, sets his stance, and fires back, nine quick shots. Seven of them go wild—two of them strike the man in the thigh, and then the belly.

He staggers, falls; Stewart fires again, and his head opens up. He falls over.

In the control room, Darrow yawns.

"Sucks for him," says Ives.

"This was a man without a plan," says Army Man on the screen. "Right there. He had the tools, but he didn't have the responsibility, or the reaction time, to do what he needed to do with them."

"Concerning," says Stacey Robwright.

Back on the RISON screen, Rison appears to have gotten lost. He's in some maintenance hallway in the mall, and he's just running around with a grenade in one hand and a pistol in the other.

"I thought these guys had familiarity with the location," says McDean.

"You can't design away stupid," says Perry amiably.

As Rison runs around, panting, he comes upon a janitor pushing a rolling garbage can around.

Rison stops. The janitor stares at him.

Rison says, "Uhh . . . Excuse me, uh . . ."

"Oh, Jesus Christ," says McDean.

Andrews cackles wickedly in the back of the control room.

"Could you tell me, uh . . ." says Rison. "Uh, where should I go from . . ."

The janitor turns and sprints away.

Rison says, "Aw, shit!" He raises his pistol and fires, catching the man in the shin as he turns a corner.

Rison runs after, following him. He turns the corner and finds the janitor sitting on the ground, screaming in fear, chattering away in some language—Polish, maybe—and finally saying, "*No, no, no, no!*"

"This is why," says Bowder's voice on the screen, "you

should arm *everyone* at your facility."

"Fuck!" says Rison. "Fuck, fuck!" He raises his pistol—the bodycam footage is shuddering and quaking, so they switch to a drone shot—and he hesitates. Then he screams, maybe in rage, maybe in fear, and starts shooting at the man, six shots, one after the other. Fountains of blood burble up from the janitor's face, neck, torso, arms. He falls over and begins shaking, one arm mindlessly scratching at the wall, his legs kicking back and forth.

"There's the chicken dance," says Perry from the sitter pit. "Musta caught him in the skull . . . Yep! There it is. Right above the temple. Fucker's sprung a slow leak!" His tone is genial, appreciative.

"Fuck," says Rison on the screen, staring down at the dying man. "Jesus." Then Rison hears Bonnan's AL-18 out beyond, and he runs back down the hall and out to the main area.

"We should note," says Bowder, "that studies show most enemy agents will *not* hesitate this much or be this compassionate. Rison wasn't sure what to do—but most enemy agents, like Stewart, like Bonnan . . . well, they won't think twice or ask questions."

McDean turns around. "Numbers!" he shouts.

Ives and Andrews shake their heads, amazed. "Through the roof," says Ives. "Through the fucking *roof*!"

"Really?" says McDean. "Even for another mall?"

"Doesn't seem to be hurting anyone's feelings," says Ives. "We've got ninety-three million tuned in. Most via smart TVs, but lots of social media feeds, some people logging directly on to the ONT site . . ."

McDean is amazed—and then he thinks of Perseph. Kruse said to activate when the audience had reached its peak. "And still climbing?"

"Still climbing."

"The *moment* that thing starts to plateau, you tell me, okay?"

"Got it, boss," says Ives.

McDean looks back at the screen. Bonnan has turned onto a major passageway, about sixty feet wide, and it's full of scattering people. They know what's happening now—they see the drones, they know this is a *Vigilance.* People are fleeing into stores; some have been trampled and are crawling away. There's an incredible amount of screaming—and then it's joined by a sudden chorus of phones ringing, one after another, *beep*s and *boop*s and *chime*s and *ding*s.

"Just lifted the comms ban," says Neal from the eval pit. "Tons of people calling in now, trying to warn them."

"Too late," says Darrow.

All the ringing phones also make it a lot harder to hide—which is the point.

Bonnan is surprisingly good at this: he moves slowly, carefully, taking aim and using short bursts. The AL-18 really is just a fucking amazing weapon, minimizing kick-back and concentrating the burst. A teenage girl drops, then a twelve-year-old boy, then an old man who's just sitting on the ground crying, *bang, bang, bang.*

"This is why you make sure to train with the best possible equipment," narrates Bowder on the screen. "Look at how he's moving down the hallway. Look at how he's staying out of sight lines, maximizing his view of the field while minimizing his exposure. Remember, the bad guys *will* be ready, and they'll have access to such remarkable weapon systems as the AL-18 just like you."

"That's an excellent reminder, Bob, thank you," says Robwright. "If these people had weapon systems comparable to the AL-18, would they be prepared enough?"

"They'd have a much higher chance for survival, Stacey," says Bob. "*Much* higher."

McDean, though, is very aware that carrying around an AL-18 in public is liable to make anyone think a *Vigilance* is taking place, and blow you away in hopes of getting a cool five million. Ives is very good at suppressing those news stories, because Wayne Hogget Hopper is, of course, a huge investor in the company that manufactures the AL-18. It's critical to maintain the weapon's branding as a token that prevents death rather than inviting it.

"Oh!" says Gramins on the screen. "Looks like ... Looks like Bonnan has a challenger!"

A police officer has taken cover behind a row of trash cans. His Klimke is in his hand. He waits for a break in the action, then pops up and fires ...

He misses. This isn't huge surprise—most police officers score about a 20 percent rating when it comes to marksmanship.

But Bonnan does not miss, almost solely because his weapon is so superior to what the cop's sporting: the AL-18 saws through the trash cans instantly, and the policeman collapses to the ground.

"Not a good sign for this mall's security so far," says Robwright's voice. "Not good at all."

Delyna stares at the screens, surrounded by images of the officer lying on the ground, motionless. The cameras pour over him, taking in every angle of his death. She is struck by the galling humiliation of it all, dying alone behind a row of mall trash cans, purely for spectacle.

Someone is shouting at her. She blinks—the man in the Oklahoma hat is standing at front of the bar, snarling, "—*oors Light!*"

"What?" says Delyna, startled.

"I said give me another fucking Coors Light before I miss anything else!" he shouts. "God*damn,* girl!"

Delyna grabs the tap with shaking hands and begins to pour yet another beer. Oklahoma whirls around as there's another burst of shooting and passingly makes some comment, but all Delyna can hear is the sound of knocking at a door, and shrieks of dismay and grief.

She watches the glass fill and tries to remember where she is.

"Something interesting happening with Stewart," says Darrow from the eval pit.

"Let's check him out," says McDean.

"We now go to Stewart," says Robwright's voice, almost automatically.

The feed cuts to Stewart, who's stalking around a women's clothing store—small, upscale, very nice. The sign says it's called Epheme.

"Crank up the ad dollars from Epheme," says McDean. "Just *look* at this fucking exposure we're giving them."

"You got it," says Ives.

As Stewart stalks through the store, he pauses, thinks, and fires a couple of rounds at the checkout desk. An older woman, about sixty, gray-haired, and overweight, tumbles out from behind it, bleeding copiously from the neck.

Stewart stares at her for a moment, then walks forward to confirm she's down.

"Yep. Yep! Got a shooter in the rack!" says Darrow suddenly, excited. "Look, there! Right there!"

It's rare for Darrow to be excited about a *Vigilance*—after four or five of these, nothing really surprises you anymore—but then they see what he's pointing at: there's a twitch from a thick rack of dresses in the far back, and then the barrel of a pistol emerges, ever so slowly.

"Ohh, shit!" says Neal. "This is some fuckin' television, folks!"

For a while, nothing happens.

"Taking aim," says Darrow. "Making sure they got a clear shot . . ."

Stewart stands up, looks around the store . . .

Four shots ring out, and Stewart falls.

"Did you see that?" cries Perry from the sitter pit. "Wow!"

Almost in unison, Robwright's voice says, "Did you see that, folks? Wow. Wow!"

The drone feeds quickly establish that Stewart is not down, not out, not dead: most of the shots hit his body armor.

"Of all the times a fuckin' moron goes with the armor," says Perry, "and it actually comes in handy."

But being shot while wearing body armor is still not at all a pleasant experience. Stewart is on the ground, moaning and whimpering, and he's dropped his pistol. So, he can't react when the shooter leaps out of the rack of dresses and advances on him.

It's a woman—a young woman, about twenty-four. She's crying as she advances on Stewart, the gun trembling in her hands. She's Asian. Neal and Darrow's AIs go to work, and they quickly identify her as Phuong Dang, visiting from Chicago.

"Shit," says McDean. "*Shit!* Asian, foreign, *and* from a big city? What are the numbers like?"

"They're . . . okay," says Ives.

"Will this blunt our TMAs?"

"It might slow them down a little, yeah. Like, it's *good*—but not great."

McDean sighs. It's not that this would *hurt* them—but his job is to follow the numbers, give people what they want, and break records every time. "Go to dupe mode," he says.

"Ten-four," says Andrews.

The main feed has maintained a distant perspective on the action for this very reason: since the civilians are the hardest to prepare for, they keep to wide, unclear angles in case they need to do any live editing.

Andrews does his thing, and the big screen in the control room splits in two. They seem to be duplicates of the same feed, showing drone footage of Epheme and some ONT pundits.

But then Andrews runs a script. Both drones zoom in on the girl, and in one, the feed shows the girl as she is, Miss Phuong Dang from Chicago. But on the other, she's suddenly different: now she's a white, Irish-looking girl with dark black hair. Perfect for Indiana.

This second image is what the viewers are seeing—the other is reality. It's essentially an image overlaid on top of her—a highly advanced copy-and-paste.

"Who is that we're seeing, Bob?" asks Robwright on the screen.

"Our ONT sources say this is Miss Molly Jones," says Bowder's voice. "And isn't she *remarkable*? Look at her stance as she holds the pistol!"

"Molly Jones?" says McDean. "From the Beatles song?"

"The algo pulled it on random chance," says Ives. "I'm putting together a social media profile for her now."

"Miss Jones is visiting Daileyton from Bloomington," says Bowder on the screen. "Just complete chance that she's here today."

"Mm," says Robwright's voice. "That's why you have to be vigilant, of course. Anytime, anyplace."

"Exactly, Stacey," says Bowder.

McDean cringes. That's a little on the nose for his tastes. But his audience likes it, he knows.

McDean's team watches on the unfiltered drone feed as Miss Dang advances on Stewart, weeping and trembling and shouting in Vietnamese. Stewart coughs, looks up, and sees her. He holds up a hand, alarmed: "No! No, no, no, I'll split it with you, *I'll split it with yo*—"

"That's against the rules, pard," says Perry.

Either way, Miss Dang isn't having any of it: she screams at him in Vietnamese, and the control room's AIs, sensing the language, translate it almost instantly for the control room to read: "*Do the fuck to yourself! Do many fucks to yourself!*"

Darrow bursts out laughing. Dang is shrieking and sobbing now, her words so overwrought that the AIs can't make heads or tails of it.

"No!" screams Stewart. "*No, no, no, n—*"

She starts firing, over and over again. Some shots hit his armor. But not all—his neck is unprotected. His throat bursts open, and a nearby hanging rack of off-white bras is spattered with arterial spray.

McDean checks the viewers' feed. On that one, the white, handsome-looking Molly Jones is shooting at Stewart, screaming, "*I'm a patriot! I'm a patriot! I'm a patriot!*"

He narrows his eyes. Sometimes, he can't believe the shit that tests well with his audience.

Then, in a very weird unison, the women on both screens collapse beside the bleeding, dying Stewart, and weep hysterically.

"That," says Andrews approvingly, "was some very good tape."

"Victorious!" cries Gramins on the feed. "Victorious. Can you believe it! Can you *believe* it?"

"Amazing," says Robwright. "Simply amazing. She

passed. She did it. Miss Jones—you, more than anyone else we've seen so far—are vigilant."

"I'm pulling up her Nuuvu profile now," says Bowder's voice. "It appears Miss Jones is a *fervent* marksman. She trains, she prepares—and today, it really paid off."

McDean walks over to Ives's pit. "The real lady—Miss Dang—is a goddamn accountant," says Ives. "Barely knows how to fire a gun. She got lucky as hell."

"But you've made a profile for Jones, right?" asks McDean. "And you've made sure she likes and supports all of our advertisers?"

"Miss Jones is a very, very big fan of tactical lights," says Ives.

"Excellent."

"What are we going to do about the Vietnamese lady?" asks Ives.

McDean thinks about it. He sure as hell doesn't want to pay her the five million—such a thing would cause talk, and people might eventually realize they'd edited the feed.

But then, all kinds of people are getting killed here today. "What's Bonnan's location now?" asks McDean.

"He's about six hundred feet down the hall from her," says Darrow.

"Well. Why don't we give him a trail of breadcrumbs, then?"

The patrons of the South Tavern bar whoop and clap as the Jones girl fires round after round into the prostrate form of the shooter.

"That's how you do it, baby!" shouts one man. He pumps his fist. "That's how you *do* it!" Other exclamations include "*Pow!*" and "*Bam!*" and "*Tee Kay Oh!*"

"Look at her," says one woman. "That is some ugly crying right there. *Ugly.*"

"Bitch, like you wouldn't be sobbing your eyes out if you went through a *Vigilance,*" says her friend.

"The second I knew a *Vigilance* was going down, I'd be reaching for my makeup, not my gun," she says.

"Tough for a face to be pretty when it's got a lot of holes in it," says a man.

They stare at the sight of Miss Jones weeping hysterically on the floor—and then, abruptly, the television goes blank.

The crowd stares at the dark television screens.

"Huh?" says a woman.

"What happened?" says a man.

Finally, the man in the Oklahoma hat turns and sees

Delyna standing at the bar, shivering with rage, holding out the remote with one hand, her index finger pressing down the power button. "What the *fuck*?" he squawks, furious. "Turn it back on!"

Delyna slowly takes a breath, lowers the remote, and then stares at him, her expression calm and cool and collected. "No," she says.

McDean doesn't *like* doing the trail-of-breadcrumbs trick, of course—this is a lot of work. They'll have to create a whole bunch of generated shit for this totally fabricated Miss Jones—grieving parents, grieving siblings... Who knows. But it's better than the alternative.

Really, it's just a matter of the wrong place at the wrong time—or, more specifically, the wrong person. Foreign, female, big city, and Asian ... John McDean's Ideal Person doesn't *dislike* such a person. It's just that they just get far more excited by the idea of a local white lady as a victorious shooter—enough to generate a significant bump to the *Vigilance* target market activations.

And when it comes right down to it, you do whatever it takes to get your TMAs.

Darrow and Neal quickly hack into the phones of the dead, using an advanced drone puttering through the hallways—it just needs to get close for them to get in. Then they set up the breadcrumbs: a trail of phones that make a loud, distinctive, high-pitched beep.

They watch on the drone footage as the first beep definitely gets Bonnan's attention. He skulks over, AL-18 ready. Then the next phone beeps, and the next one—and he's drawn farther, and farther, closer and closer to Epheme.

"Oh, dear," says Robwright on the screen. "Look . . . It does look like maybe her crying has gotten Gabriel Bonnan's attention, or perhaps it was the shots."

"Classic mistake," says Army Man, always helpful. "You stay silent, you stay out of sight, and you do *not* let the situation overcome you."

Bonnan walks to the door of Epheme. He looks in, sees Miss Phuong Dang sitting on the floor, crying next to Stewart's corpse. Without any hesitation, he aims and fires. Her back bursts open in at least three or four places. She slumps over, dying, trembling, choking.

"Ohh, dear," says Robwright on the screen. "No, no! She was almost out! She almost *had* it!"

Gramins heaves a deep sigh. "What a heartbreaker. I can't believe it. What an absolute heartbreaker."

In the control room, McDean says, "Let's get hashtag RIPMollyJones trending on everything ASAP."

"Already on it, chief," says Ives. McDean watches on his tablet as massive flocks of bots and hacked accounts begin percolating, tweeting out thousands of messages instantaneously, flooding the social media feeds.

"And our advertisers are looped in?" says McDean.

"We're tied at the hip," says Ives. "They're all on board with it."

"Well, holy shit," says McDean. "Well done, gents."

"Turn it back on," says the man in the Oklahoma hat. "*Now.*"

"No," says Delyna again. She tosses the remote into the icebox behind her and slams it shut.

"We were watching that!" says a second man. This is his friend, the man who's always leaving his gun in her goddamn bathroom, the one she thinks of as a mechanic. His hands, she sees, are filthy yet again.

"And I got tired of it," says Delyna.

Oklahoma advances on the bar in a furious bantam strut. He leans over it and sticks his finger in her face. "Now, you listen," he says. "I had money riding on that episode. We all did. Now, you get that fuckin' remote out of the ice, and you turn it back on. This instant!"

Delyna stares back into his face and calmly, slowly blinks. "No," she said. "I will not."

"Do it!" says Oklahoma. He leans over farther into her area. "Do it *now*!"

"The same damn show is running in every bar in this neighborhood," says Delyna. "Every one except this one. You can take your party next door and watch it there."

She hears a shuffling series of footsteps from the kitchen. "Delyna . . ." says Raphael's voice reproachfully.

"I don't want to fucking hear it, Raphael!" she snaps, not taking her eyes off Oklahoma's face. "I am damn tired of seeing people die on my goddamn television! I've seen it enough in real life, I don't want to see it there, too!"

"Come on," says the mechanic. "Let's go."

"No!" snarls Oklahoma. "No! I had fucking *money* riding on that game. And this . . . this is disrespectful to me!"

"We need to hurry if we don't want to miss anything," says the mechanic.

"I don't think you hear me," says Oklahoma. "It's *disrespectful*!" He turns his stare back on Delyna, and she can see he's getting all pumped up now. His eyes are wide and drunk, and he's shifting uncertainly on his feet, lurching back and forth. He sticks his finger out at her again. "I don't need to take your *shit*."

"I am not giving it," says Delyna. She switches to a bloodless, formal vernacular that she learned from her father. "I am simply making a choice about the programming we are displaying at our venue for this evening. Those who disagree with the choice have ample selection elsewhere in the city."

Some of the patrons are leaving, huffy and furious. But not all—about half remain, staring at Delyna with drunken, angry eyes, seemingly catalyzed by Oklahoma's fury.

"I want to speak to your manager," says a woman behind Oklahoma.

"You are welcome to," says Delyna. "Tomorrow. He will not be in this evening."

"Give me that fucking remote!" says Oklahoma.

"No, sir," says Delyna.

"Don't you fuckin' *sir* me," he says. "Don't act like you're being respectful now! Everything about this . . . it's all about disrespecting me!"

"It is not," says Delyna. "It has nothing to do with you."

"It does," he says. "It does."

"Then it is my duty as the bartender of this establishment," she says, "to inform you that you are mistaken."

He stares at her, scandalized. "That I'm what?"

She turns and sees an order of chili cheese fries on the order counter. She picks it up, along with the beer she just poured.

"Don't you fuckin' turn your back on me!" he says.

"Again, you are mistaken," she says. She turns back around. "I was not turning my back on you. I am fulfilling an order. Who had the chili cheese fries and the Coors?"

There's a silence. Then an obese, very inebriated man in the back guiltily raises a hand.

"I will bring it to you," she says curtly. She begins to step away.

She sees the movement out of the corner of her eye. Oklahoma reaches down, grabs something, moving fast, and then suddenly the group around him disperses, stepping back *fast*. A couple of people gasp, and one man shouts, *"Watch it!"*

Delyna freezes, turns around, and sees the pistol in Oklahoma's hands, pointed directly at her head.

"Disrespectful," he says, his voice slurred. "This is *disrespectful*, is what this is."

"That situation's resolved," says McDean merrily. "Why don't we show the exits?"

"Can do, boss," says Darrow.

On the screen, the viewers' feed switches to Stacey Robwright's face, concerned and slightly disgusted. "And it does sound like we have an unfortunately large number of people trying to escape the environment . . . Let's take a look." The feed switches to drone video of a small crowd of people, mostly families, desperately hammering on the twenty-foot-high walls of bulletproof glass that have barricaded the exits of the mall. ONT security contractors look on from behind the walls, their faces fixed in the blank, dull expressions of someone being paid a lot of money not to think or feel. "Look at these people—trying to escape!" says Robwright's voice contemptuously. "They turn and run, like cowards, rather than prepare themselves and fight!"

"We always have this happen, Stacey," says Gramins's voice, "and it always surprises me how many of them there are."

The video of the terrified mall customers shrinks to become a thumbnail. The main feed changes to Gramins, Robwright, and Army Man sharing a large couch together, hunched forward like someone watching a tense football game.

"I mean, think about it," says Robwright. "They could have been like Molly Jones. They could have fought back. They could have been victorious, even for a moment. But they chose not to."

"It really does make you think about what's going on in America," says Army Man. "It really does."

McDean doesn't feel great about how this one worked out. Usually, they show the exits after a *successful* victory: the goal is to make the audience feel anxious but also superior to these people who are trying to flee. You prove it can be done—then you show people who didn't even try. It's just all compromised by their having to take out Miss Dang.

But he did the math: the TMAs for having an Asian lady take out a shooter were far, far lower than the TMAs for seeing the exits after a compromised civilian victory. It would have seriously damaged his aggregate scores.

"Audience growth rate?" asks McDean.

"Holding steady," says Ives.

"Jesus. Amazing. Let's roll some ads."

"Ten-four," says Andrews.

Robwright faces the camera. She smiles glamorously. "We're going to take a quick break and be right back."

The ads roll.

"Sir," says Delyna quietly. She has to clear her throat. Her mouth is dry, her ears are suddenly hot, and all the world is faint and distant. "Sir, I am not sure what . . ."

"You *shut up*!" shouts Oklahoma, shoving the pistol forward. "You shut up! I am tired, I am *damn* sick and tired of being disrespected all the time!"

She swallows. She feels like she's about to pass out, and she has to struggle to stay standing. "Sir . . ."

"Scott," says the mechanic. "Scotty, what the hell are you doing?"

"I am *fixing* this," says Oklahoma. "I'm fixing what's wrong! Don't you see it? Don't you see how these people are? How they get at you?"

Delyna thinks, *Who is "these people"?* But she's smart enough to keep quiet.

The crowd is alarmed, but they don't seem particularly offended by all this. They appear to be waffling back and forth between interest and irritation: they're not sure if they like what they're seeing, but they're willing to keep watching. They are just curious spectators in this horrifying moment in Delyna's life.

"It is my *right*," says Oklahoma. "It . . . It is my *right* as a citizen to have my voice heard!"

Delyna struggles with her bewilderment. "And watching the channel you want to watch in some dive-ass bar is how you make your voice heard?" she asks, genuinely astonished.

"It was a *Vigilance*!" he shouts. "You can't turn that off! We got to watch, we *got* to!"

She is so agog at this line of argument that she forgets the gun in his hand. "Sir," she says forcefully, "it is a *television show*."

"It was a *Vigilance*," says a woman in the back. "What kind of person turns that off?"

Delyna looks around and realizes she's losing the crowd. These people might very well let him shoot her, or even approve of his doing so.

"All our lives, we get attacked," says Oklahoma. "Every day, our way of life comes under siege. We are always having to defend ourselves. We are *always* having to fight for what's right. But I'm sick of it. I am willing to be a warrior for *truth*."

Delyna's head is spinning. It's surreal. She thinks she heard those lines once on *The O'Donley Effect*.

The crowd is nodding. She sees Raphael withdrawing from the order counter, eager to get out of the line of fire.

She realizes she needs to do something.

Shit, she thinks. *What do these people want to hear?*

She looks at the crowd again, shaking with fear. She faintly realizes that these people are watching because they expect to see something akin to the stories they see on television all the time: there is a bad actor, there is a hero, and then there is violence, resolving the issue.

How do I change the story? How do I get myself the hell out of this?

She has an idea. She's heard plenty of ONT in her life, and she quickly cobbles together some stolen lines.

"I'm," she says haltingly, "I'm ... just a bartender. I came here to go to work. That's all. I'm ... I'm trying to run things as I have always run them, as I choose to run them. That's *my* right. That's my right as a citizen."

"We have to watch," Oklahoma says. "We *have* to. We got to stay alert!"

The crowd nods. "We do," says a woman. "How are we going to stay safe?"

"But I'm not safe," says Delyna. She looks at the gun. "Am I?"

"You ... you *chose* to put yourself here," says Oklahoma angrily.

"Noooo, no no no," says Delyna. "The one making the choice here is you. You're the one choosing to stick a gun in my goddamn face."

There's a flicker of emotion in the crowd at that.

"I didn't hurt anyone," says Oklahoma. "*You're* the one who hurt us!"

"I did not," she says. "You think you're the good guy here? That you're the one putting things to rights? Imagine if you walked into any other place and saw a man pointing a gun at the clerk and making demands! Why wouldn't you think he was a thief, a murderer? Why *wouldn't* he be the bad guy?"

She feels the crowd considering that.

"I ain't a damn thief!" he snarls.

"Not yet," she says. "But if I give in here, why wouldn't you ask for my till? Why not my goddamn tips? What's keeping you from pointing that thing at everyone else in here and demanding their wallets, their jewelry, their lives? If you're willing to do it to me, why not them?"

The crowd exchanges a glance.

Holy shit, she thinks. *Is this working?*

"I ain't a damn thief!" he says again, louder.

"What you are is a screaming man with a gun in an American bar," she says. "And I bet if any one of these people pulled iron on you and gunned you down, they'd be considered heroes for doing it."

Now the crowd is *very* intrigued. She isn't even sure if

"pulled iron" is an actual cowboy phrase, but it sounds cowboy enough.

Oklahoma feels the crowd turning on him. "You shut up!" he cries.

"If this were a *Vigilance*," she says, "who do you think the active would be? And who'd be the hero? Are you so sure it'd be you?"

Oklahoma glances around and licks his lip. "You . . . You be quiet."

But it's too late. The crowd starts moving.

A woman at the far table frantically pulls her hand out of her purse, holding a pistol. She points it at Oklahoma, her hand wobbling like the gun is too heavy for her wrist. "Listen, you . . . you mother*fucker*," she says, nervously excited. "You put that dang thing down!"

Oh, shit, thinks Delyna.

Oklahoma wheels and points the gun at her. "W . . . What?" he says.

The obese, inebriated man who ordered the chili fries fumbles to produce his weapon. To Delyna's horror, it's some kind of fully automatic pistol. "Don't . . ." He pauses to belch. "Don't you point that thing at her!" he says.

Everyone stares at one another for a moment.

Please, no one else take out a gun, she thinks.

Then the mechanic steps back and awkwardly reaches

for his holster. He's surprised to find it's missing. He looks around and cries, "What? No! Fuck, *fuck*! Not again!"

"Stop," says Delyna. "Please, just—"

"Stop it!" screams Oklahoma. "Stop it! Everyone stop it!"

"Put it down!" screams the woman.

"Put it away!" shouts the drunk man with the automatic pistol.

Another man reaches for his gun.

Delyna stares in horror as her gambit continues to go wildly awry. She'd just wanted Oklahoma to relent, to put his gun away out of fear someone might shoot—but she'd never thought everyone would eagerly *fight* to be that someone.

They all want to be heroes, she thinks, dismayed. *They all want to be dumbass heroes in their dumbass stories!*

Oklahoma is panicking now. He stares at the many, many firearms now pointed at him.

"You stupid bitch," he says quietly.

Delyna sees that he's desperate—and she knows desperate men do very stupid things.

He grimaces and says, "You stupid black bi—"

It's at this moment that the bathroom door slams open, and Randy—drunk-ass, homeless, sad-eyed Randy—comes staggering out. He's holding something in his right hand. To her dismay, Delyna sees it's a Klimke pistol.

The crowd turns to stare at him, surprised.

"Hey!" shouts the mechanic. "That's mine!"

Randy leans this way and that, a classic drunk's struggle with equilibrium. "Check this shit out!" he shouts, holding it up. "Think this thing's loade—"

He pulls the trigger. The gun goes off. A bottle of vodka explodes on the wall behind Delyna.

Without another thought, Delyna dives behind the bar.

The South Tavern erupts with the harsh, brittle cracks of gunfire. Delyna doesn't have the mind to scream, she just rolls up in a ball on the sticky, beer-soaked floor and covers her head, trying to make herself as compact as possible. She can hear people screaming and stumbling around, she can feel the reverberations in the floor as the bullets strike the walls, she can feel dust drift down to her as they chew into the ceiling. One sound is especially predominant, a raw, hyperactive chattering of gunfire from what she suspects is the fat man's automatic pistol.

She dimly realizes that now she is screaming, shrieking at the top of her lungs as the gunshots go on, and on, and on.

And then, finally, they cease.

She lies on the floor, ears ringing, her heart fluttering

madly. She's smart enough to stop screaming, just in case Oklahoma is still alive and willing to kill her. She just lies on the floor, listening.

All she hears is a dull coughing and something dripping—all else is silence.

Delyna slowly sits up, still listening closely. Nothing. She crawls to the edge of the bar and peeks out.

The South Tavern is a tattered, ruined mess. Bodies lie everywhere, drooping over tables and chairs or prostrate on the floor. Glasses have exploded into twinkling shards that stretch across the floor.

Everyone, it seems, is dead or at the very least dying. Oklahoma is perhaps the most dead: there is not much left of his head or, indeed, even his chest. It seems everyone was very excited to shoot him. The woman who pulled her gun from her purse is lying across a table: she apparently took some kind of advanced round in the stomach, and her intestines droop from the edge like festoons of garland. The mechanic is sitting up against the wall with a tiny, perfect hole drilled beside his nose. Poor Randy is dead as well, having taken a bullet in the belly just above his crotch, and another in the chest. The fat man with the automatic pistol is still alive but obviously not for long: he's taken three, four, maybe five hits to his torso. It's clear he did the majority of the damage, and he's still trying to do more: he is still waving his pistol at the bar, his finger still squeezing the trigger.

Delyna watches him until finally his arm falls and the gun clatters to the ground.

She hears a rustling behind her and sees Raphael's face peeking over the order counter.

"God *damn*," he says softly. "God damn, Delyna. Girl . . . Girl, why didn't you just turn it back on? Why?"

She stands up. She thinks for a moment, then goes and grabs her purse from the office. "I'm gone," she says.

It takes him a moment to understand her words. "You what?"

"I'm gone," she says. "For the night. Forever. Tell Martin I quit." She starts walking to the back door. "And remind him of what my *fucking name is*!" she shouts over her shoulder.

McDean stares at the ads as they wash over him.

This is a different set from the previous advertisements: they're gorgeous, wonderful, calibrated creations, all winsome nostalgia and beatific calm. His ads feature old Chevrolet trucks with wooden beds, the kind that haven't been made in over one hundred years; they feature milkmen, and mailmen, and firefighters, and policemen who look like they came out of a comic book from the 1930s; families strolling through pecan groves; kids going to diners and getting a fucking malt milkshake, kids putting pennies in piggy banks; librarians with beehives and horn-rim glasses; people wearing brimmed hats and then tipping the hats to each other and saying "yes, ma'am," and "no, ma'am." It's just a giant nostalgia enema, glimpses of an America that, if it ever even existed, is nearly a century old by now.

And his audience fucking loves it. He watches on his tablet as his TMAs climb, and climb, and climb.

It's a psychological trick that McDean developed and refined: he gives them an oasis of the achingly familiar amidst this rush of modern carnage. It isn't enough to dilute the audience's anxiety, but it gives them a moment to catch their breath.

He nods as he watches the data on his template—Pareto charts and bar charts and multiple regressions and ARIMA models. It's a wonderful, beautiful symphony of data, all brought about by his marketing innovations.

Striking that balance of terror and relief has been a learning experience for McDean. When they first started *Vigilance,* they went all in on fear and terror, and that worked at first—somewhat. But trying to figure out which images and experiences goosed his core demographic—and his Ideal Person, his most valuable viewer—was strange.

At first, he went with dead children: images of them, audio of the school shootings, news footage from school shootings, and so on. He'd thought this would activate their most protective instincts, sure, but the main reason why he went with dead children was that just they had *so much* material of it—for although America doesn't manufacture much anymore, it sure as hell makes a lot of dead kids: children shot at schools, in the home, at the playgrounds; shot by cops, by themselves, by their parents, by each other; just heaps and heaps of little angelic bodies, all perforated with bullet holes, all still and cold and perfect.

Surely, he thought at the time, this would evoke the

desired biochemical reactions in his target audience. Surely, this would alarm them into never turning away.

And yet their reaction had been . . . muted.

He's seen it a lot since, and it's puzzled him every time: John McDean's Ideal Person is just strangely unaffected by the sight of dead children. It simply doesn't do it for them anymore, if it ever did.

It bothers him. He knows it shouldn't—usually, he just forgets about the stats that have such low R-squared scores—but it just *does*.

Why are these grandmas and grandpas and mothers and fathers just so fucking *indifferent* to the sight of so many children in harm's way? Why?

He's developed a theory about this, a crude one, a strange one—but one that he thinks comes close.

To witness youth in this America is, in a way, to know that the world is failing. It's failing in lots of ways: the reproduction rate has plummeted; the immigration rate is a net negative; the government is bankrupt; lots of America is either sinking into the sea or burning like kindling; and on, and on, and on.

So, when they look upon the young and see how miserable and terrified and despairing they are, some part of the older generation's brains *must* realize that they were the ones who'd been the stewards of America during all of this—and that they'd just fucking blown it.

And they *had* blown it, McDean supposes. The wheels have come off the economy two, three, four times. The melting Arctic is belching methane into the atmosphere. McDean can't even keep track of how many wars they are in these days, or how long they'dvebeen going on for. And China has just blown by everyone, turning into some scientific marvel, engineering super soldiers, seeding the stratosphere with sulfates to slow the changing climate, and even starting to terraform fucking Mars, for Christ's sake.

The older generations had sat back and just watched all that happen, or even *made* it happen. That is a fact, and they know it, though they might not want to admit it. Yet when they saw their unhappy, dwindling progeny, the evidence was undeniable.

So, what did they do?

They destroyed the evidence—or they allowed it to be destroyed.

It makes sense, he thinks, in an Oedipal kind of way: if your children represent all of your most massive failings, you naturally come to subconsciously resent them, to hate them, to desire their punishment.

And that was what had happened—each time the younger generations had said, "This is hurting us," the elders had cried, "You dumb, ungrateful kids! You think *that's* hurting you? We'll just do it twice as much, then!"

And so they had. Even when it hurt them too, when it

hurt *everyone,* they still did it. All these strange, inexplicable, self-inflicted wounds, seemingly done for the sheer, selfish pride of it all ... For McDean, a marketing man who feels obligated to understand his audience, it is still largely a mystery. His grotesque theory is the only thing that comes close.

Eventually, the *Vigilance* team gave up on dead kids and switched to armed minorities, and that worked out just fine. It is an old warhorse—show John McDean's Ideal Person a dead kid, and he shrugs. Show him an image of a black man with a gun (or a Mexican, or a Muslim), and all the needles just dance like ballerinas.

He watches on the big screen as an ad rolls depicting a tricked-out Cadillac with tinted windows, cruising down a suburban street. The windows roll down a crack, and a pair of eyes peer out suspiciously. The race of the person is unclear, but they're not white. Then the protagonist of the ad—Joe McBlandGuy—puts on a pair of augmented-reality glasses, and the advanced lenses read the license plate on the Cadillac, identify all the crimes it's been associated with, and assigns it a threat level ...

It's a generated ad, of course: a dream whipped up by machines to terrify the elderly with a vision of an America that doesn't really exist.

It suddenly strikes McDean that this is a very odd way to make a living—but at least it's a living.

"Chief," says Ives, standing in the media pit. "Chief, chief! We just broke it, we just broke it!"

"Broke what?" asks McDean.

"The TMAs!" says Ives. "Fucking hell! You broke your TMA records *again*!"

The control room breaks out into whoops. McDean tries to grin but can't quite bring himself to do it. He clears his throat. "Audience rate is still climbing?"

"It's slowing but not plateaued yet," says Ives.

So, no Perseph—not yet at least. "All right," says McDean quietly. "All right."

His phone vibrates softly. He looks at it—a message: *u ready?*

He mentions something about the bathroom and walks away.

· · ·

The door reads his biometrics, clicks open, and he walks in. He stands in his private bathroom, unlocks his phone—finger, face, breath—and sends a message to Tabitha: *ready. what the hell app is this?*

Her response: *apoidea*

He sends back: *what the fuck? do i need a dictionary*

to run this app

Her: *you work in tech, you know they go for bullshit greek names*

Him: *fine fine*

He finds it on the app store. This is totally against company protocol and should be impossible, but he got Darrow to crack his phone for him ages ago.

He installs the app and asks her: *username?*

She replies: *honeygirl*

Him: *jesus. ok*

He finds her on the app. They connect. Then he waits.

Finally his phone vibrates, and the app says: INCOMING MESSAGE. He hits the OK button. The screen goes black and says: PLEASE PLACE DEVICE SCREEN UP.

"Huh," he says. He does so.

The screen flickers—and then, to his shock, a tiny, mostly nude Tabitha suddenly appears to be standing on his phone, wearing nothing but white socks and pink tennis shoes.

His mouth falls open. "Holy shit," he says.

"Hey!" she says. Her voice comes from his phone, he can tell. "Hi! I can see you." She points at him with two fingers. "Can you see *me*?" She points at herself with two fingers.

He looks at her, craning his neck from side to side. "Uhhhh. Yes."

She laughs, giddy, and twirls. "Whaddya think?"

"How . . . How the fuck does this work?"

"Don't be stupid, Johnny. It's an optical illusion. Look at the phone from the side."

He does so, looking at it from the very edge. She appears to vanish. "Oh," he says.

"It's super hard to get the angles right—like, when I look at you, I'm really looking at nothing—which is what my friend Madeline told me would happen. But . . . can you see this?" She does some kind of dance move, kicking her leg so high, her kneecap touches the side of her torso. "And *this*?" She twirls again, leg high in the air. It's impressive; he forgot she did dance in high school.

He hears explosions and screams from the main room. Something's just happened on *Vigilance*. Something bad.

She lowers her leg. "What was that?"

"You're not watching?"

"No, dumbass, I had to get all this set up. I don't usually do my hair and wear makeup to just be naked, you know."

"It's nothing," he says hoarsely. He holds his hands out to her, as if feeling a radiant warmth from her tiny, frail, flickering body.

"What are you doing?" she says.

"Nothing. Please keep dancing."

"Do you want me to dance? Or do you want me to do *this*?" She does the splits.

"Oh my God," he moans.

"And this?"

"Jesus . . ."

"And . . . let me see . . . I'm not sure if I can pull this one off . . ."

He shudders, overcome, and unzips his pants. Then, serenaded by the distant sounds of screams, gunfire, and death, John McDean frantically, desperately masturbates to the faint, pale vision of youth twirling about on his phone.

Delyna walks through empty, quiet city streets. There are no cars, no buses, no pedestrians, no nothing.

But then, there wouldn't be. There's a *Vigilance* on, after all, and most of the world shuts down when that happens.

She's still shaking, still trembling. She still hears the gunfire in her mind. She has a curious desire to jump into a hole and hide, hide from the smell of the burning propellant and the smoking wood, worming her way deeper into the earth to avoid the violence she'd been running from all her life yet was never able to truly escape.

A light rain begins to fall. She has no umbrella. She stops and looks up at the sky.

Once, it snowed during this time of year in the city, but it never does anymore. It will never snow here again in the remaining duration of the human species, however long that is. She knows this for a fact. Remembering it fills her with a curious, aching loneliness.

She sees the ONT tower in the distance, the three letters glowing a clean, clear white. Then she lowers her eyes and sees a restaurant full of people, all the customers standing around a handful of television screens.

What an easy thing it is, to make Americans destroy ourselves, she thinks. *You just have to make a spectacle out of it.*

She walks on into the city.

There's a pounding on the bathroom door. "Boss?" says Ives's voice. "You asked when we were plateauing on numbers. We're just about there."

"Got it," calls McDean. He's finished and mostly cleaned up by now, but he still enjoys just looking at Tabitha.

The two of them exchange a glance. Tabitha smiles wickedly and holds a finger to her lips. He smiles and does the same. Then she does something with her hands—probably fiddling with her phone—and she vanishes.

McDean exits. Ives is waiting in the hall, looking calm. He probably thinks McDean was doing drugs in there—which he was, in a way. Tabitha definitely alters the chemicals in his brain. "We're sure?" asks McDean.

"We're sure," says Ives. "And get this—Bonnan's still going. He's approaching the record for most kills. The cops have him hunkered down in an AirWei store."

"A fucking tech store, huh?" says McDean as they walk down the halls. "Well. More ad revenue. What happened to Rison?"

"Blew himself up," says Ives. "Along with a *lot* of cops. That's probably why Bonnan's still going. Rison was upstairs and had an angle on the cops as they were going to advance on Bonnan. He tossed one grenade right into them, but the other . . . eh. Held onto it too long."

"How many cops still standing?"

"Four. Bonnan's been tagged in the shoulder, but he's still going. AL-18s, man. All the other shit just can't compete."

McDean walks back into the pits and takes stock of the situation. It's a shootout—classic stuff—but he knows it can get boring if it goes on for too long. Army Man—for the first time, McDean sees his name is supposed to be Admiral McDonough—is animatedly describing how he'd take Bonnan out.

"*Wild Bill Bonnan* is trending on Nuuvu," says Ives. "I didn't make *that* one up."

"Because it's fucking stupid?" asks McDean.

"Yeah."

His phone vibrates again. His heart swoops as he checks it, but it's not Tabitha again—it's Kruse. "Fuck," he mutters. He composes himself and answers it, saying, "Hello, Mr. Kruse."

"Hallo, John. I understand you are about to activate Perseph."

"Yes, sir."

"Well. I would like you to know that while Perseph is active, there will be filters in place in the control room so you and your people do not feel its effects."

"Uhh. Oh. Really?"

"Well, yes. If you saw it, you would be . . . well. Pretty useless for a while. You would just keep watching—which is the point. This is very advanced stuff, far more advanced than anything China has."

McDean very much fucking doubts that. "I see, sir. Is . . . Is there a process that I need to go through to make this all happen?"

"No, no. I have been in communication with Andrews. It is a simple permission he needs to run. I just wanted you to be aware—while Perseph is active, do *not*, say, look at the ONT platform on your phone, or something of that sort."

This disturbs the ever-living shit out of him. "Is there anything else I need to know, sir?" he asks, exasperated.

"I suppose we will find out!" says Kruse chipperly. "Goodbye, John."

There's a click, and the phone goes dead.

McDean looks at the main feed. The AirWei store has rows and rows of tables, all covered with tablets, phones, VR and AR sets, and so on, though they've all been pretty much destroyed by the gunfire. It's dark, but the drones have night vision, so he can see Bonnan crouching behind the back left desk. There's an open door to his right, but it probably just goes into the store's server rooms or broom closet.

"Do I run it?" asks Andrews.

"Audience growth is fading," says Ives. "Not yet zero—but it's fading."

"Do I run this thing, sir?" asks Andrews. His tone is somewhat insolent.

McDean thinks of one of his ads: the soldier holding the little boy, shining a light into the darkness. He thinks of Tabitha, rendered in pale pinks and reds, twirling on his phone. He thinks of Phuong Dang sitting on the floor and crying.

"Fuck it," says McDean. "Yeah. Go ahead."

Andrews clicks his mouse a few times. And then . . .

Nothing. Nothing seems to change. Bonnan is still hunkered down. The cops are still taking potshots at him.

But Ives says, "*Whoa.*"

"*Whoa,* what?" says McDean.

Ives stares at his monitors, his mouth agape. "All our numbers . . . Like, *all* of them. They're holding perfectly, perfectly steady. Look." He swivels his screen around and shows McDean his charts: the lines are all flat, perfectly, perfectly flat. It's like there's an error in the program. "Totally static. Like a frozen heart, mid-beat."

"Is this . . . correct?" says McDean.

"I think so," says Ives. "Like . . . Who knows?"

"Holy *shit*," says Andrews.

McDean turns around. "What now?" he asks.

"Well . . . I can't see *what* Perseph is doing," says Andrews. "Like, I can't see the results, what the viewer sees. But I can see the processing power that it's eating up, and . . ." He shakes his head. "I've never seen anything require this before. Maybe if I were, like, trying to map the entire surface of the earth, and project it in the sky, beside the moon or some shit."

"But . . . But what *is* it doing?" asks McDean, frustrated.

"Beats me," says Andrews. "A *lot* of something."

"Whatever it's doing," says Ives, "people can't look away."

McDean turns back to the main feed. Bonnan's still there. Cops still taking potshots.

He imagines his audience staring at their screens, unable to turn away or blink or move because of . . . something. Something this artificial mind is doing to them, having been taught, in a way, by McDean himself.

But what did he teach it to do? What is it showing them?

Black boxes inside of black boxes inside of black boxes.

"So, now what?" asks Darrow. "We just . . . keep going?"

"Until our audience fucking dies?" asks Neal.

"Wouldn't take long," says Perry with a laugh. He spits into his cup.

"We just . . . complete the *Vigilance*," says McDean, feeling curiously helpless.

They all look at each other.

"All right," says Darrow. "Can do, boss."

"Give me some better eyes on Bonnan," says McDean. "And this isn't great television, frankly. A dude holed up with a bunch of broken phones . . . I don't want to watch that."

"Sure thing," says Neal. "What's the move?"

McDean frankly isn't sure. If Perseph is doing what Kruse says it should be doing, then it doesn't really matter what they do.

"Let's goose him," says McDean. "Use one of the drones in there to set off a minor flash. We need to create some action. Get the conflict going aga—"

"He's moving!" says Darrow.

McDean watches as Bonnan readies himself, then pops up and fires three quick bursts at the cops. He dives over the checkout desk and dashes into the open door in the back room—the one McDean assumed went to the server room.

"Where the hell's this kid think he's going?" asks Perry.

"Follow him," says McDean. "The show drones can remote into anything, right? If so, we'll need to be ready. I don't want him, I don't know, fucking with their servers or anything."

"Kid's from Iowa," says Perry. "A hacker he ain't."

"Yes, sir," says Darrow. "The show drones can remote in if they get close. But let's see . . ."

The tiny drone floats forward, into the open door. It's dark inside, but the night vision adjusts . . . and McDean sees something very strange.

Bonnan is standing quietly to the side, firearm lowered, like he's waiting for something. Sitting before him is a curious device: it looks like a large, black halo on black metal stilts. There's a thick cord running from the back of the halo, and it's plugged into the servers . . . but the servers look very unusual. They don't, in other words, look like the sort of servers that a goddamn mall tech shop should have.

Neal and Darrow shoot to their feet. "Oh my *God!*" screams Neal, a real, genuine scream of terror.

"No way, no *fucking* way!" shouts Darrow.

Everyone's shocked to see them react this way. Most of the time, they never react at all.

"What the hell?" says Perry. "What's wrong with you tw—"

Then the main feed goes dark.

Then all the rest of the feeds go dark.

Delyna is about to walk across the bridge when she hears a harsh *crack*.

She stops.

She knows that sound. She just heard a hell of a lot of it, after all.

She looks around for the gunfire—she thinks it was behind her. Then she hears another *crack*—but this one is across the river.

Then another, and another, and another... Gunfire from the apartment buildings, from the alleys, from the streets. Some of it even appears to be coming from the restaurant at the corner.

"What the hell?" she whispers.

The *Vigilance* crew stares at their darkened feeds. Some of their computers seem to be working, but anything that has anything to do with watching *Vigilance* is dead.

"What was that?" says McDean. "What the hell was *that*?"

"It was . . . it was a Shandian," says Neal. He sounds shaken. "I . . . I think. Right? Wasn't it?"

"It was," says Darrow hoarsely. "I've only seen the specs. But I think it was."

"The fuck is a Shandian?" asks Perry.

"It's an . . . an antenna," says Neal. "Made by Zhōngháng Kuang. Chinese tech company."

There's a silence.

"An antenna?" says Ives. "That's it?"

"Like bunny ears?" asks Perry.

"No, dickbags!" says Darrow angrily. "It's like a Wi-Fi antenna turned up to a million! It's basically an AI bomb! It fools anything looking for a connection to automatically route into it! Once the connection's made, it leaps up the chain like lightning, jumping from device to device. Some Pakistani terrorists used one in India. Drove it into a military base, turned it on. The place started firing missiles like a goddamn firework."

Another silence as everyone considers this.

"So . . . when your drone got close to the Shandian," says McDean slowly, "then it would have automatically connected to it . . . and then leapt up the chain, to . . . here?"

Darrow slowly exhales. "It would have *tried* to. But the defensive AIs here are top-of-the-line, NSA stuff. Unless we were compromised from within somehow, it should have been stopped or hopefully slowed. Alarms would have gone off, at the very least! But I didn't hear a single one!"

"Then why are our feeds dark?" asks Andrews.

"I don't fucking know!" shouts Darrow.

"Can you do something?" asks Ives.

"I frankly don't want to fucking touch anything!" says Darrow. "If it's really in here, the Shandian AIs will notice me doing something. It's very, very, very sma—"

Then, in the distance, they hear a *pop*.

And another *pop*.

And another, and another.

"Is that in the building?" says Perry.

"It's outside . . . I think," says Neal. "It's small-arms fire. Someone shooting."

More *pops*. And more, and more, and more.

"Sounds like ... like a *lot* of people shooting," says Ives.

"Yes, it does," says Darrow tersely.

"Can we go look?" says Andrews.

"Look where? Out the windows?" asks McDean. "Is that safe?"

"It's not close," says Neal. Another *pop*. "Well. Not *that* close. It should be all right."

Quietly, they all troop down the halls and out the front desk area to the glass windows. They're on the forty-third floor of the ONT building, which is locked down tight as a drum with *Vigilance* going on.

They line up at the windows. They see figures running around in the lamp-lit streets below. Lots of them. And they're shooting at each other.

It's not a war, or a battle or something—not as far as McDean can tell ... Rather, it's a fucking free-for-all. Everyone is shooting at everyone, shotguns, rifles, pistols, and assault rifles, just total mass chaos.

"What the fuck," whispers Perry. "What the *hell* ..."

"Is it war?" asks Andrews, nervous. "Have we been invaded?"

"It's ... It's like a riot, or something," says Neal. "I'm not seeing any tactics, any ... anything. Just shooting."

There's a silence filled only by the sound of gunfire.

Then Andrews whispers: "Is it Perseph?"

"What?" asks McDean.

"Did . . . Did Perseph do this?" he asks. "Did it do this to . . . to everyone?"

They stare at each other.

"What do you mean, *do this*?" asks Perry. "What's *this*?"

"I don't know!" says Andrews. "Drive people crazy!"

"Maybe he's right," says McDean. "I'm calling Kruse. Now." Then he pauses, and glances at Neal and Darrow. "Can I? Or will this thing . . . the Shandian . . . will it know?"

"Chief, we are out of our league here," says Neal. "Do whatever you think is going to fucking work."

McDean pulls out his phone and does his little ritual—finger, face, breath—and unlocks it and calls Kruse.

It rings. And rings. And rings.

"Is he answering?" says Andrews.

"Does it fucking look like he's answering?" says Perry.

Then McDean hears a click, and a sunny, bubbly female voice says: "Hello, John!"

McDean stares into space, shocked to hear her voice. *Tabitha?*

"Wh . . . What?" he says, dimly.

"How are things going for you, John?" says her voice. "Probably not very good, I'm guessing."

"I . . ." He considers what to say, since his entire crew

is watching him. "I was trying to call . . ."

"Oh, I know who you were trying to call. Kruse isn't going to answer, though. He's not going to answer for a very long time. Maybe *all* time, really."

McDean swallows. He can hear his blood pounding in his ears. "What's going on?"

"You know what's going on," says Tabitha's voice. "Or you have an idea. Something went wrong with Perseph, yeah? Probably right after your drone got close to the Shăndiàn." She pronounces it with a perfect Mandarin accent. "Now . . . is that *really* the question you want to ask right now?"

He feels sick and faint. Somehow, he manages to stay on his feet. "What . . . What's your name?" he asks softly.

"Chief?" says Perry. "Uh . . . Who are you talking to?"

"Oh," she says. "Well. It's not Tabitha. But you're pretty accustomed to that. You generate all kinds of fake stuff all the time, don't you? Images, sounds, websites . . . See, in China, they can fabricate *real* things. Faces. Voices. Bodies. They can sculpt and re-form the human body to an amazing degree, John. Say, if you wanted to make someone look like just the *perfect* person to someone else—like the marketing director of a news slash entertainment corporation—they have systems that can figure out what that perfect person looks like, and then change you to look like that.

You guys make pictures. They make stuff that's *real*."

"You . . . You work for the Chinese?" he asks hoarsely.

"Shit," mutters Neal. "Shit!"

"I work for lots of people," she says, suddenly solemn. "You might not think it now, but I work for the American people. I've been looking for a way to change things for a long, long time. It wasn't until the Chinese got sick and tired of your ships in the South China Sea that they reached out to me."

"What?" he says numbly. "Ships?"

A pause. Then she bursts out laughing. "Holy shit, John! Did you *really* not know? There's a giant international incident happening right now! The Chinese have been threatening war for *days*. I thought you guys were a news company! I thought it was your job to report on stuff!"

"What's happening?" asks Perry. "What's going on?"

Andrews looks McDean over. "His face suggests something . . . very bad."

"It was easy enough," says her voice—whoever she is. "We knew Kruse was developing some kind of subliminal AI for you all. So, we just needed some plants. Your AIs aren't as smart as you think—it was easy to feed them the right information to get them to pick the mall. Like, it scored *super* high on the target optimization map, right? Really, really high? And then we had to get you to pick the right person to stick in there. So, we crafted Bonnan—he's an associate of mine, you know. We marketed him for you personally. Iowa, Nazi, tattoos, sociopath—a good villain. He needed to put on a good show, build up a big audience, and then take you to the Shăndiàn."

He shuts his eyes. "And you."

"And me."

"You were marketed for me too."

"I was."

"Face. Body. History."

"Yes."

"And when I downloaded that goddamn app . . ."

"Yes. While I danced for you and you jacked off, your phone uploaded a worm that killed all the defensive AIs at ONT. So, the Shăndiàn was able to get in. We altered Perseph. And we told it to send out a signal . . ."

"A signal to what?" he whispers.

"A signal to do what you've always told America to do. To be vigilant. But—against *everyone.*"

Delyna stares, terrified, as a man emerges from his building with an assault rifle. He screams something incomprehensible—just wordless, mad shrieking, it seems—and opens up on the restaurant directly next door, pouring bullets into the families inside.

But they aren't just sitting there: the families within are shooting back ... and they're also apparently shooting at each other. People who'd previously been sitting and eating together simultaneously rip out firearms and just start shooting wildly.

Delyna watches as a mother pulls a handgun from her bag, presses it to the side of her infant son's head, and pulls the trigger.

"Oh my *God!*" screams Delyna.

A bullet strikes the window behind her, shattering it. Sobbing in terror, she turns and sprints away.

McDean listens as the pops outside increase. It's like the entire city is filled with gunfire.

"Oh my God," he moans. He's shaking now. "Why?"

"Why what?" says her voice. "Why do this? I told you, the Chinese have been threatening war. This is much more effective than a nuclear weapon, you know. All the structures stay safe, and the people who weren't watching—they might be okay."

"No, I mean . . . Why are you telling me this?"

"Why? Well. I guess I just want you to *know*. To know that, at the end of the day, the Chinese and, hell, the world—they didn't really have to do anything. They weren't the threat. They weren't the opponent. *You* were. *You* people put the systems in place. *You* people built the story. *You* people put the weapons into everyone's hands. We barely had to do anything. You did it all to yourselves!"

He shuts his eyes. "Tabitha . . ."

"Who the fuck is Tabitha?" asks Darrow.

"America is dead, John," says her voice. "Not tonight, though. It died a long time ago. You people smothered it in its bed, then tried to dress up its corpse so it looked like it was alive. It needed to go, John. The forest was rotten and sick. Better to burn it to the ground and have it start over again. Fresh and new—and devoid of people like you."

"What the fuck are they *saying*, McDean?" shouts Neal.

"Ahh. Say hi to Neal for me!" says her voice. "Oh, and you may want to check the security cameras."

"The security cameras!" chokes McDean. "Now!"

They dash back into the control room. Neal hits a few keys and brings up the ONT camera feeds. They stare, horrified, as a team of armored operatives storm into the ONT lobby, quickly take out the guards, and make for the stairs.

"Fuck!" screams Darrow. "Fuck, fuck!"

"Sorry," says her voice. "We can't leave witnesses. I told them just to let Perseph do to you what it was doing to America, but—the Chinese are very thorough. They didn't want to leave that up to chance."

"You . . . You . . . you *bitch*!" screams McDean at her. "How can you do this, how can you do this?"

"He's fucking useless," says Neal. "Let's get to the lockers."

"Hell yeah," says Perry.

"You could have done anything else," says her voice.

"You were smart and powerful. You understood people. You could have helped them. But instead, you played to their worst instincts. Just for money. Just for money, John. Just for a little bit of money."

There is a *click,* and she is gone.

McDean stands there, dazed, holding the phone. He's vaguely aware of Neal and Darrow hauling out weapons—AL-18s, of course, provided by Hopper—and handing them out to the crew. "There's only one way they can get in here," says Darrow. "One way—that entrance." He points. "Stairs or elevator, they gotta go through there. And we're going to make them pay. We do this smart, do this carefully, and we might, just *might* get out of this alive."

"We've done this a thousand times," says Perry. "A million. We know shootings more than anyone else." He looks like he's getting ready to live his private fantasy. "We got the tools, we got the know-how. Let's make this happen."

"Oorah!" says Neal. "Build barricades, now—now!" He starts giving out orders.

But McDean isn't listening. He's thinking.

Because now he knows this has always been a scam—and it probably still *is* a scam. And John McDean, Director of Marketing, Master of the Universe, knows a hell of a lot about scams.

He runs out the hallway, toward the stairs and the windows beyond. "What the hell?" says Perry. "What are you *doing*?"

"Man's gone nuts," says Neal.

McDean dashes up to the windows and peers out at the city. There's the gunfire below, sure, but everything else is still. Except . . .

Then he sees them. Four smooth, gray forms drifting through the skies toward them. They look like teardrops, or the chrysalises of butterflies.

"Oh, God," he says, swallowing. He considers rushing back in to tell them to run, to go, go, go—but that would take time.

Time he could use to run away himself. And besides, they could think he's a fucking Chinese commando and shoot him.

John McDean flings open the door to the stairs and runs down.

He leaps down the stairs, jumping from floor to floor. His heart is hammering in his chest, his head's faint, his legs are buzzing, but he keeps jumping, running, tumbling, falling . . .

It's about on the tenth floor when he hears the explosions. The whole building shakes, dust starts filtering down from the ceiling, and he wonders if the building's going to collapse. He fumbles down farther, leaping and stumbling down the stairs. The explosions above him keep going on, and on, and on.

Miraculously, he makes it to the lobby floor. The guards out front are missing or dead—shot by someone, anyone. The windows are peppered with bullet spray, frosted with cracks. He sees people darting through the streets, shrieking incoherently and shooting at one another.

"Oh, God," he moans. "Oh, Jesus."

Another explosion above. He's not sure the building's going to stay standing. He remembers the loading dock out back, where the maids bring in all the laundry. He staggers through the darkened, empty lobby, bursting through door after door, until he finds the way out.

He cracks the last door open. No one on the loading dock. Another explosion above, and he makes a break for it, sprinting forward into the alley, then down another alley. It ends in a chain link fence. Beyond it is a massive, flooded storm-drain riverbed. Sobbing, he climbs over the fence, hauls himself forward, and dives into the filthy, reeking water.

He swims, unsure where he's going. He looks back and sees the four massive war drones still circling the ONT building. The floor he was just on—the floor that Darrow and the rest of his crew were probably hunkered down in—is a flaming ruin.

He knew the video of the goddamn commandos was

fake. It was just the sort of thing he'd do while running *Vigilance*. Tabitha and whoever the hell she worked for—they just wanted to keep them all in one place.

McDean swims, and swims, and swims through the filthy water until he comes to a storm drain. He hauls himself up and perches in the round mouth of the corrugated metal tunnel. From here he can see the streets on the banks above. He can see people running back and forth, shooting, screaming, bellowing like animals. Something's on fire in the distance—he can see the smoke unscrolling into the sky. A young black woman in a yellow shirt is trying to climb over the fence to get down to the river, but she's hit once, twice, and she falls back to the ground. He hears a child crying nearby, shrieking in terror. Then there's a burst of gunshots, and he doesn't hear the crying anymore.

Rocking back and forth in the drain, John McDean begins to weep. Then he curls up, presses his palms to his ears, and tries to block out the growing sounds of gunfire.

About the Author

Josh Brewster Photography

ROBERT JACKSON BENNETT is a two-time award winner of the Shirley Jackson Award for Best Novel, an Edgar Award winner for Best Paperback Original, and the recipient of the 2010 Sydney J. Bounds Award for Best Newcomer and a Philip K. Dick Award Citation of Excellence. *City of Stairs* was shortlisted for the Locus Award and the World Fantasy Award. *City of Blades* was a finalist for the 2015 World Fantasy, Locus, and British Fantasy Awards. The Divine Cities trilogy was nominated for a Hugo Award for Best Series. His latest book, *Foundryside,* is in stores now. Robert lives in Austin with his wife and large sons.

TOR·COM

Science fiction. Fantasy. The universe.

And related subjects.

*

More than just a publisher's website, *Tor.com*
is a venue for **original fiction, comics,** and
discussion of the entire field of SF and fantasy,
in all media and from all sources. Visit our site
today — and join the conversation yourself.